ALAN GIBBONS

Ganging Up

CollinsEducational

An imprint of HarperCollinsPublishers

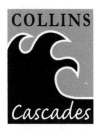

Ganging Up

ALAN GIBBONS

Cascades consultants:
John Mannion, Head of English at Elliott School, Wandsworth
Sheena Davies, Head of English at Bishopsbriggs High School,
  Glasgow
Adrian Jackson, Advisory Teacher for English
Geoff Fox, Lecturer at the University of Exeter School of
  Education, and a National Curriculum Advisor

Other titles in the Collins *Cascades* series that you might enjoy:

Space Demons   GILLIAN RUBINSTEIN

When Andrew Hayford's dad brings a computer game called
Space Demons back from Japan, a deadly battle with sinister
forces begins.
ISBN 000 330083 8

Grinny   NICHOLAS FISK

This funny, frightening book is in the form of Tim Carpenter's
diary, and describes the extraordinary things that start to
happen when Great Aunt Emma, or Grinny, comes to stay.
ISBN 000 330020 X

Elidor   ALAN GARNER

Elidor is a twilight world almost destroyed by fear and
darkness. When four Manchester children find themselves
there, they realise that only they can save Elidor, but gradually
the evil starts to invade their own lives.
ISBN 000 330087 0

Black Harverst   ANN PILLING

A family on holiday in Ireland awaken the ghosts of the Irish
famine. This horror story is moving and atmospheric, raising
issues of famine both today and in the past.
ISBN 000 330063 3

For further information, please call 0141 306 3455

COLLINS
Cascades

To Bethany

Published by Collins Educational,
an imprint of HarperCollins*Publishers* Ltd,
77–85 Fulham Palace Road, London W6 8JB

www.**Collins**Education.com
On-line Support for Schools and Colleges

First published in Great Britain by Orion Children's Books a division
of Orion Publishing Group 1995
Reprinted 1999 (twice), 2001

ISBN 0 00 330 339 X

British Library Cataloguing in Publication Data

A catalogue record for this book is available from the British Library.

Cover design by Ken Vail Graphic Design, Cambridge.
Printed in China

Contents

ONE

Action

SOMETIMES I THOUGHT IT WAS ME AND GERRY AGAINST the world – other times I *knew* it was.

Soccer brought us together – literally. Gerry McEvilly was chasing his ball the day he cannoned into me in Walton Hall Park. The collision led to a game. Dad and son, Ryans against McEvillys. We lost 2 – 1. That was six years ago. Since then Gerry and I have been inseparable. We've had loads of nicknames over the years: Tom and Jerry, Batman and Robin, Tonto and the Lone Ranger. None of them stuck, but the idea did. We were a Gang of Two – three if you count the football we were forever knocking around – and no matter what we would stick together.

Sure, we had our moments. Who doesn't? When we were five I knocked out a couple of his teeth with the garden swing. When we were seven he gave me a black eye with a Mutant Turtle. None of it made any difference. We were mates, and by the time we reached Year Six we were the school team's twin strikers. I was built like an anorexic pipe cleaner so I went for the high balls. Gerry was shorter but tough and wiry with a blistering turn of speed. Apart we could be dangerous. Together we were dynamite.

We proved it one showery April evening after school. Goof had arranged a training session down at the Sports Centre.

'If we want to put English Martyrs on the map,' he told us, 'then we've got to work at it.'

'What does he mean *we*?' Gerry grumbled.

'For goodness' sake,' Goof complained as we split into two teams, 'can't you two play on opposite sides just for once?'

The answer was no.

Goof gave in as usual and we did the business – as usual. I scored twice. Gerry got his hat trick.

'OK lads,' said Goof peeling off his track suit jacket. 'Let's see if we can even things up a bit.'

'That's not fair, Mr Scarry,' said Tony Crawford. 'That's six onto five and you're a grown up.'

Not just a grown up, he was also a teacher and the coach of the school team, so late tackles were out.

'Well?' Gerry asked.

'Well what?' I answered. 'We'll still thrash them.'

Gerry grinned. 'Of course we will.'

It wasn't quite that easy, but we did eventually get the better of them. I side-stepped Goof's clumsy challenge and rolled the ball to Gerry. He winked and gleefully tapped it home. The second goal was also down to me and Ger. This time Gerry beat Goof and Neil Delaney. I hit his pass on the volley.

'Good strike,' said Goof.

'Good strike,' echoed a voice. It was mocking, really sarcastic. I looked up.

'Bride Lane,' I murmured.

'That's all we need,' grumbled Phil Smith. 'White-washed twice by Chip and Dale here, then they turn up.'

There was no love lost between English Martyrs and

Bride Lane. The two schools were less than half a mile apart and both drew kids from the giant North City estate, but you wouldn't know we had anything in common. At least once a week they would turn up in force at our school gates, making us run the gauntlet to get home.

'Well, what have we here?' called their leader. 'I didn't know you could train chimps to play football.'

The bad blood between the two schools went back as far as anybody could remember. My mum once tried to explain how it all started but I think it was just a few bullies who wanted somebody to hate. The Bride Lane gang's main mouth was Graham Skinner. He was older than us and went to North City Comp. As a school it made a good war zone.

'Why don't you come out to play?' he called.

That was the signal for the Bride Lane boys to start shaking and booting the high wire fence that surrounded the five-a-side pitch.

'Hey,' Goof shouted. 'Give over!'

It was the turn of Graham's kid brother Danny to say his piece.

'Make us,' he taunted, tugging at the fence with all his might. 'Go on slaphead, make us.'

The word *slaphead* set Goof's teeth on edge. He was very sensitive about his bald patch.

'Clear off!' yelled Gerry, moving towards the fence. Neil Delaney had been ready to have a go himself, but to everyone's suprise Gerry beat him to it.

'Don't rise to it, Ger,' I whispered. 'That's what they want.'

I didn't know what had got into Gerry lately. Like me, he'd always steered well clear of the gangs.

'Shut it,' warned Danny Skinner. 'We can easily find out where you live.'

'Yeah yeah,' said Neil. 'You've got us shaking in our boots.'

'Stop it, Neil,' said Goof. 'And you, Gerry. I'll have a word with the Sports Centre staff.'

When he returned a few seconds later with two track-suited members of staff, the Bride Lane kids were already retreating across the playing field.

'We'll be seeing you,' shouted Danny Skinner. 'Soon.'

'Not if I see you first,' retorted Gerry.

'Knock it off, will you?' I complained. 'I've got to walk home with you, remember. Do you want to get us done over?'

'I can handle it,' said Gerry.

'Handle it?' I sneered. 'I'd like to see you handle Graham Skinner.'

We were interrupted by Goof.

'That was none too bright, Gerry,' he told him. 'I expect better from the team captain.'

'They asked for it,' said Gerry sullenly.

'Maybe so,' said Goof, self-consciously stroking his bald patch. 'But you've got to learn to rise above that sort of nonsense. I've seen too many good lads from round here slide into trouble. You can do better, Gerry.'

Gerry gave Goof a cool stare. What *had* got into him? He was usually so easy-going.

'Anyway,' sighed Goof, 'bright and early tomorrow lads. A good performance against Northfield and we're in the semi-finals.'

Neil Delaney shook his head. We didn't need reminding.

Everybody was really fired up for the game. We were convinced the Inter-School trophy had our name on it.

'You did well there, Gerry,' said Neil as we turned right out of the Sports Centre and walked home across the park. 'I always thought you were teacher's pet. I didn't know you had it in you.'

I glanced at the sallow, crop-haired eleven-year-old beside me. I didn't like him – never had. He was always in trouble for one thing or another – fighting usually. Everybody on North City knew the Delaneys, and not for their charitable works either. They and the Skinners had coined the market in bullying, vandalism and downright rottenness. What's more, the two families had been carrying on a vendetta since the year dot.

'It's just a pity that fence kept us apart,' said Gerry. 'I don't know who Danny Skinner thinks he is.'

I knew exactly who Danny Skinner thought he was – a cross between Arnold Schwarzenegger and Attila the Hun, and his older brother Graham was worse!

'I tell you what, Gerry,' said Neil quietly. 'If you want action stick with me and you'll get it.'

'How do you mean?' asked Gerry.

'You'll see,' said Neil, tapping the side of his nose with his forefinger. 'You'll see.'

TWO

A tale of two houses

'WHAT'S GOT INTO YOU?' I DEMANDED AS WE LEFT Neil at the top of his street.

'You what?' asked Gerry.

'You,' I replied. 'It's bad enough shouting the odds at Bride Lane, but what are you doing listening to Neil Delaney? I thought you had more sense.'

'Then you thought wrong,' said Gerry. 'Anyway, have you finished moaning yet?'

'I'm not moaning,' I protested. 'I just . . .'

With a loud snort of impatience Gerry marched ahead through a swirl of wind-tossed litter. I finally decided to leave well alone. There was no talking to him that evening. It was something I'd noticed recently. He was up and down like a yo-yo. You never knew when he'd lose his temper over the slightest thing.

'Got any plans?' he asked as we reached his front gate.

I shook my head. 'Nothing special,' I told him. 'We could go over to ours. I've got a new game.'

'What's it called?'

'Star Raiders,' I told him. 'Have you got it?'

'No.'

I waited at the front door while Gerry dropped off his sports kit. He only lived ten minutes walk from my house but there was a world of difference between the two sides of the estate. Down this end – the frontline between Martyrs and Bride Lane territory – there were boarded-up, graffiti-marked houses in nearly every road and dogs were roaming everywhere.

By then it had begun to rain steadily. Under the massing clouds, the skyline was dominated by two tower blocks that were being cleared of tenants ready for demolition. People talked knowingly of what went on in the stairwells. I wouldn't say North City was tough, but even the pit bulls went round in pairs.

'Do you want to come in for a minute?' asked Gerry.

I followed him into the living-room.

'Hello, Mr McEvilly,' I said, seeing Gerry's dad sitting in front of the television watching the soccer preview.

'Hello John,' he grunted.

I could hardly believe the change in him over the last couple of months. He used to be really funny, and always had a story to tell. The moment you walked in the house he would switch off the TV and ask you about things: how the team was doing, what my dad was getting up to, how the twins were, that sort of thing. Not any more. His eyes didn't even leave the screen. My dad said it all started when the work on the building sites dried up.

'Can I go to John's?' Gerry asked.

'Ask your mum,' said his dad.

'Mum,' Gerry called up the stairs. 'Can I go to John's?'

'What are you pestering me for?' shouted Gerry's mum. 'I've got Susie and Kieran in the bath. Ask your dad.'

Gerry rolled his eyes. 'Come on,' he said. 'We won't get any sense out of them tonight.'

As we closed the living-room door I could hear Mrs McEvilly yelling at Susie and Kieran.

'Is it always like that?' I asked.

'No,' said Gerry. 'You caught them in a good mood.'

I knew it was meant as a joke but Gerry wasn't laughing.

'Hang on,' I murmured as we reached the street corner. 'What's up?'

'Can't you see?' I nodded in the direction of Graham and Danny Skinner. They were hanging around a burned-out car with their mates.

'I bet they came looking for us,' said Gerry. 'This isn't Bride Lane territory. Follow me. We'll go round the back way.'

He led me through the overgrown garden of a boarded-up house at the end of his Close and through a hole in the fence. Skirting the rubbish-strewn brook which ran along the back of the houses, we reached the Salvation Army car park and cut through onto the main road.

'This rain's getting heavier,' I said.

'You won't shrink, you know,' said Gerry.

I pulled my hood up. I didn't care what Gerry said, I didn't like getting wet. Wet's for ducks.

'Raining, is it?' asked Dad when he answered the door.

'No,' I said. 'It's just a rumour.'

'So I suppose you want to come in?'

'We wouldn't mind.'

'What are the bricks for anyway?' I asked, pointing to the pile on the front path.

'I'm going to build a barbecue,' said Dad.

'You?'

'Yes, me.'

I shook my head. Somehow Dad and DIY didn't mix.

'In you come then,' said Dad, 'but slip your trainers off first. Your mum will go mad if you walk a load of mud in.'

We sat down and pulled off our shoes. As I hung up my new coat, I glanced at Gerry. He was completely drenched. The shoulders of his thin cotton jacket were stained dark with the downpour, and his hair was plastered to his head. His trainers squelched as he removed them. Even at the best of times Gerry was to fashion what egg and chips is to Cordon Bleu cookery. But today he looked even more tatty than usual. You wouldn't think those clothes dressed English Martyrs' – and probably Liverpool schools' – best player.

'So how's the Scousers' Pele?' asked Dad.

'Not so bad,' said Gerry. 'We turned on the style tonight.'

'That right, John?' asked Dad.

'Not half,' I told him. 'We won even though Goof played for the other side.'

'That's Mr Scarry to you,' said Dad. 'Anyway, keep the noise down. We're getting the twins ready for bed.'

I could hear my twin sisters squealing in the living-room as Mum chased after them with their pyjamas.

'It's a madhouse,' I observed.

'You don't know when you're well off,' said Gerry as Dad went back into the living-rrom.'

I led the way upstairs.

'You try first,' I told him as I pushed a game into the computer console. 'It takes a bit before you get the hang of it.'

'Do your mum and dad like you?' Gerry asked out of the blue, immediately after being obliterated in the asteroid belt for the third time.

I took over and blasted off from Moonbase.

'That's a funny question,' I said.

'But do they?'

'I suppose so,' I told him, dodging an alien starfighter. 'I've never thought about it.'

'Mine don't,' sighed Gerry, stretching out on my bed. 'They hate me.'

'Don't be soft,' I scoffed. 'They can't hate you.'

'Why not?'

I was entering the asteroid belt and needed to concentrate.

'Because,'

'Because what?'

That did it. I lost a wing to rogue meteors and spiralled out of control before exploding.

'Now look what you've done!' I shouted. 'I've never bombed out on Level Two before.'

'I didn't do anything,' protested Gerry.

'You wouldn't shut your trap.'

'It's only a stupid game,' he snapped. 'Do you want me to go?'

He stamped to the door.

'Hang on,' I said. 'Of course I don't want you to go.'

Gerry hesitated in the doorway.

'Carry on with what you were saying,' I told him.

'Are you going to listen?'

'I'm listening. Look, this is me listening.' I stood to attention with my hands over my ears.

Gerry grinned. 'Wipe that daft look off your face and I will.'

I ran my palm over my face. 'There you are,' I said. 'One daft looked wiped off my face.'

'They do hate me, you know. I heard them arguing last night.'

'What were they arguing about?'

'The usual,' said Gerry. 'It's always money. Mum was saying she didn't know how they'd afford new school shoes for me. Then do you know what Dad said?'

'No.'

'That we cost them a fortune. He said they'd be all right if it wasn't for the kids.'

'He doesn't mean it.'

'How do you know?' Gerry asked glumly. 'I can't do anything right. Sometimes he even hits me. Does your dad hit you?'

'Not really,' I admitted. 'He's shaken me about a couple of times, but he doesn't really hit me.'

'Mine hits me just for talking,' said Gerry.

'You're kidding!'

'He does. Not all the time but I asked Mum something yesterday when the footy was on and he belted me. You can't talk to him. He flies off the handle at the slightest thing.'

I stared across at Gerry. I'd never seen him so miserable.

'You know what makes it worse?' Gerry continued. 'It's always me he picks on, never Susie and Kieran. There must be something wrong with me.'

'Of course there's nothing wrong with you,' I said. 'You're the oldest, that's all. It's the same with me.'

Gerry just stared at his feet.

'He used to be a good laugh,' I said. 'What's up with him?'

'Beats me,' said Gerry. 'All I know is he's all right one minute and ranting and raving the next. Mum's nearly as bad. They're always ganging up on me.'

Just then there was a knock on the door.

'Do you want to give the twins a goodnight kiss?' asked Mum.

I opened the door.

'Hiya Don,' said Rachel. She never could say John.

'Hiya Derry,' said Megan. She had the same problem with Gerry.

'It's Gerry,' said Gerry. 'G-G-G.'

'Derry,' chorused my little sisters.

'Close enough,' said Gerry giving each of the girls a peck on the cheek.

'Kiss,' said Megan.

'Kiss,' said Rachel.

'OK, OK,' I said. 'I'll give you one.'

'Come on girls,' said Mum shepherding them along the landing. 'Straight to sleep and no climbing out of the cot.'

I watched Mum tucking them in.

'Try to be quiet,' she said, closing the door to the girls' room.

'Sure Mum,' I said as she went downstairs.

'How do you think we'll do tomorrow?' asked Gerry, brightening.

'Against Northfield?' I asked. 'They shouldn't give us much trouble.'

'That's what I think,' said Gerry. 'We're going to win the Inter-Schools this year, you know.'

Gerry was a different person when he was talking about football. It was his lifeline. Mention footy and all the worries of the world vanished from view.

'We'd better win,' I told him. 'My dad's got a bet on with a bloke at work. His son goes to Bride Lane. Anyway, do you want a can?' I asked, by way of changing the subject. 'We've got Coke or Tab.'

'Tab,' said Gerry.

I ran downstairs. Mum met me in the hallway. She'd been inspecting Gerry's trainers.

'Have you seen the state of these?' she whispered.

I nodded. 'A bit mucky, aren't they?'

'A bit! They're ripe. I don't know how his mother can send him out like that . . .'

Mum stopped dead. She was looking over my shoulder.

I spun round. It was Gerry. He must have started following me downstairs and was standing about half-way, listening to our conversation. It was the expression on his face which struck me. He looked crestfallen, even ashamed. We stared at each other for a couple of moments before he hurried down the last few stairs and started pulling on his trainers.

'I'll be off now,' he mumbled.

'You don't have to,' said Mum. She looked nearly as sick as Gerry. His clear blue eyes met hers.

'I do,' he replied. He opened the door and stepped out into the rain.

'Oh John,' Mum groaned. 'I *am* sorry. I didn't mean it to sound like that.'

'Forget it,' I said, before jogging back upstairs. I listened for a few seconds to check that Mum was busy, then crept into my parents' room. You could see the whole Close from their window.

Easing back the net curtain, I peered out, There was Gerry wandering along the pavement, kicking a drink can before him. My heart sank. Though I couldn't think why I felt sick at heart. I had the oddest feeling. It wasn't just Mum who'd let him down; it was me too.

THREE

Missing

D AD REVVED THE ENGINE IMPATIENTLY.
'He's not coming, you know.'

'Can't we give him five more minutes?' I pleaded. 'He never misses a home game. You know that.'

It was true. Rain or shine, Gerry and I had been going to see Liverpool play every other Saturday for five years. It had been a foursome at first, but Gerry's dad stopped going soon after he was laid off.

'No spare cash,' he'd said, but that didn't stop Gerry going. So far, they'd always scraped enough together to send him through the hallowed Shankly gates.

'I can't give him any longer,' said Dad. 'I've got to call in at the newsagents on the way. That delivery girl missed us this morning.'

'Why don't we call in at Gerry's on the way?' I asked.

'Sorry, John lad,' said Dad. 'We're going and that's that.'

Dad selected first, indicated and pulled away. I looked behind just to check that Gerry wasn't running down the road, but it was deserted. 'I wonder where he is,' I said.

'Didn't he mention the match this morning?' asked Dad.

'No.'

I thought back to the game against Northfield. We'd made heavy weather of our 3 – 2 win.

'There's something wrong with Gerry,' I told Dad, 'He didn't score this morning. He didn't even come close.'

'You hit a cracker though, didn't you?' asked Dad.

My heart swelled with pride.

It had been good having him there to watch me score the winner. He'd missed a couple of games through shift work.

'It wasn't bad, was it?' I chuckled.

The smile drained from my face as I remembered Gerry. He'd fluffed chances he usually put away without a moment's hesitation and lacked his usual pace. His heart just hadn't been in it.

'Didn't you notice anything about Gerry?' I asked.

'Everybody has their off days,' said Dad as he pulled up outside the newsagents. 'Even Gerry. Anyway, let's sort out my paper.'

'I'm thirsty,' I announced as we walked through the door.

'Get a couple of cans then,' said Dad. 'Good morning Mr Stewart. I'm afraid that new girl missed me again.'

The newsagent shook his head. 'She'll get used to it,' he said. Apologizing for the mix-up with the paper, he folded it and handed it over the counter.

'Anything else, Mr Ryan?'

'Yes,' said Dad. 'Our John's getting a few cans.'

I closed the cabinet door and turned towards them, dropping dad's Lilt. As I bent down to pick it up I came face to foot with a pair of cherry red Doc Martens. They belonged to Steve Delaney. He was Neil's older brother and one of the cocks of the estate with a reputation as a hardcase. He wasn't alone either. Dean Brewer was with him.

They gave me the creeps. You know the sort: ingrowing

hair, calloused knuckles from dragging their fists along the ground, and brains the size of peas.

'Hey grandad,' said Steve. 'Give us twenty Regal.'

'The name is Mr Stewart,' said the newsagent. 'And I'm not your grandad.'

'OK,' said Dean. 'So give us the ciggies *Mr Stewart*.'

Mr Stewart gave him a long, hard stare. 'How old are you?'

'Old enough,' said Steve.

'I doubt it,' said Mr Stewart. 'I'm sorry lads, I think you're under age.'

'Give us the ciggies, grandad,' repeated Steve.

Mr Stewart pointed to the door. 'I think you'd better leave.'

Dean pushed a few newspapers onto the floor. 'Serve us,' he snapped, 'and pronto.'

'I've got the right to refuse service,' said Mr Stewart, 'and that's just what I'm doing.'

Steve leaned across the counter. 'You can't do that!'

'You heard the man,' said Dad. 'Now, are you leaving or do I have to escort you to the door?'

That was all I needed; Dad upsetting one of the Delaneys. I didn't fancy Neil bouncing on my head.

'Keep your nose out,' yelled Dean. 'This has got nothing to do with you.'

Dad tucked the rolled newspaper in the back pocket of his jeans and took a step forward. 'Want to bet?' he asked.

I cringed. Dad seemed to think Liverpool was a kind of Dodge City that needed cleaning up and he'd obviously decided that this town wasn't big enough for the three of them.

'That's all right, Mr Ryan,' said Mr Stewart anxiously. 'I don't want any trouble.'

Dad hesitated, wondering what to do next. Dean broke the stalemate by shoving all the magazines off a wire rack and making a run for it.

I breathed a sigh of relief.

'Young thugs,' Dad snorted as they shouted abuse from a distance.

'Forget it,' said Mr Stewart, taking the money for the drinks and the paper.

'Does this happen often?' Dad asked.

'I can handle it,' said Mr Stewart.

'You shouldn't have to,' said Dad. 'Yobs like that give North City a bad name.'

It was hard to give it a good one. People who lived in the neighbouring streets called it Beirut on account of the semi-derelict tower blocks and the boarded-up houses on the east side of the estate, and maybe – just maybe – because of the undeclared war between the Skinners and the Delaneys.

'Anyway,' said Dad. 'We'd better be off.'

'Anfield?' asked Mr Stewart.

'Where else?' said Dad with a smile.

We drove to the car park off Priory Road and walked to the ground. While Dad bought a programme I looked around the milling supporters. I suppose I was half-expecting to see Gerry making his way through the crowd towards me, but there was no sign of him. Missing a home game – this was serious.

FOUR

Selling a dummy

'GIVE US A KICK, GERRY LAD.'
The shout came from Neil Delaney. He was leaning against the railings with his brother Steve. I recognized Dean Brewer and one or two others but there were five or six unfamiliar faces among the gang kicking their heels by the park entrance.

'Come on, give us a kick.'

'Let's clear off,' I said in a nervous whisper.

'Hey thicko,' said Steve, punching the ball out of Gerry's hands. 'You heard our Neil. Give him a kick.'

'Not got the kids with you tonight?' Neil taunted.

He knew exactly how to get under Gerry's skin. Mrs McEvilly had taken to dumping Susie and Kieran on Gerry when she'd had enough of them. That's why he'd missed the Liverpool – Arsenal match. Everybody made fun of him about it. Babysitting again, Gerry lad?

Gerry ran his eyes over the dozen lads facing him and thought better of talking back. 'No.' he replied shortly. 'Not tonight.'

'Come on Neil,' shouted Steve. 'Let's show them how it's done.'

He rolled the ball to his younger brother and pounced on the return pass.

'Come on then,' he told Gerry. 'Try to take it off me.'

Gerry's face brightened. Life had been dealing him a pretty lousy hand lately, but when it came to football he was a star. Every bit of pride, all the frustrated energy went into the game. Steve was tapping the ball from foot to foot. He really fancied himself.

'Well,' he said. 'What are you waiting for?'

He punted the ball ahead of him and prepared to give chase, but he was in for a surprise. Gerry scampered forward and took the ball on his instep, skipped over Steve's flailing tackle and left the teenager sprawling on the gravel path. As I watched Gerry standing hands on hips waiting for round two of the duel, I remembered what my dad once said: 'That lad's got the makings of a professional. If he doesn't get into trouble first, he could be on Liverpool's books.'

I sometimes wondered whether Dad was exagerrating, but Gerry had ability all right. He had everything: the speed, the skills, the shimmy. Give him a football and something special happened, a fire lit inside him.

'Cheeky little rat!' gasped Steve, but his voice betrayed a touch of grudging admiration.

'Why don't you try to take it back off me?' said Gerry.

Steve glanced at Neil. 'Cocky, isn't he?'

'He's going to bring the Inter-schools trophy to English Martyrs,' Neil told him. 'And he's a cert for Liverpool schoolboys.'

'Liverpool schoolboys, eh?' Steve still wasn't wholly impressed. He obviously thought his age gave him the edge over a mere eleven-year-old. Without warning, he suddenly lunged at Gerry, but Gerry was ready and danced away grinning broadly. 'You'll have to do better than that,' he called.

'I'll have you,' said Steve, setting off after Gerry. His face was red, and he was breathing heavily.

'Now you see it,' said Gerry, poking the ball forward. Steve lashed at it, grabbing for Gerry's sleeve at the same time.

'Now you don't.' Gerry jinked first right then left and turned to face a humiliated Steve Delaney.

'OK,' said Steve. 'You win.' He stretched out a hand.

What's this, I thought, Steve Delaney being a good sport? It'll be raining candy floss next!

Gerry took his hand.

'Now!' snapped Steve, twisting Gerry's arm roughly up his back. 'Don't try to be clever with me again – ever. Got that?'

Gerry was twisting and struggling to break free, but his fighting didn't match his football.

'I said, got that?' Steve repeated, gripping Gerry by the jaw and squeezing hard.

'Yes, all right,' cried Gerry. 'I've got it, just let go.'

Steve shoved him to the ground.

'He's good though, isn't he?' said Dean, picking up the football.

'Yes,' agreed Steve. 'Not bad at all. It's just a pity about the big mouth.'

Gerry nursed his sore arm and glared at Steve. I just hoped he had the sense not to say anything stupid.

Steve took the ball from Dean, 'Fancy a game?' he asked.

'Sure,' said Gerry, the anger slipping away at the thought of a kick-about. 'Why not?' With that, he unzipped his jacket and set it down on the grass as a goal post.

'No, not here,' said Steve. 'We'll go in the yard at Bride Lane.'

'OK,' said Gerry, picking up his jacket. 'Bride Lane it is.'

'You're not going, are you?' I asked, appalled.

'Of course I am,' Gerry replied. 'I fancy a game of footy.'

'Don't be daft,' I retorted. 'They've got a different game in mind.'

'Maybe I fancy a spot of that, too,' said Gerry.

I couldn't believe my ears. There had been a time when Gerry thought the gangs were for mugs, now here he was itching for a fight.

'Are you coming, Gerry?' shouted Neil.

Gerry waved to the departing group, 'I won't be a minute.' He turned towards me. 'What's up, John? Lost your bottle?'

'But they're going on to Bride Lane's patch.'

'That's right,' said Gerry, 'And if the Skinners show they'll get what they deserve for the other night.'

'Come on Gerry,' I pleaded. 'Let's go home.'

'Go home if you want to,' he said. 'I'm going to Bride Lane with them.'

I watched helplessly as he jogged after the gang. I looked at my watch: it was nearly eight o'clock. There would be murder if I got home later than half-past.

'Gerry,' I murmured. 'You really are a pain.'

I caught up with the gang on the corner of Talbot Avenue.

'Oh, you've come along after all, have you?' snorted Gerry.

'Is this a mate of yours?' asked Dean.

Gerry stared at me hard. 'Yes,' he replied. 'I suppose so. Why?'

'His old man wants to watch himself,' explained Dean, 'We had a row with him in Stewpot's shop.'

'I don't know what you're hanging round with him for,' Steve told Gerry. 'He's a wimp.'

I said nothing. Call me what you want, but I'm a survivor. I've lived all my life on North City and I've never really been in trouble. I don't know what I expected next, but it came in the shape of a well-struck football cannoning into my face.

'Aw,' said Neil, delighted at his markmanship. 'Did that hurt?'

My face was numb and my eyes were watering. As I blinked away tears of pain I caught sight of Gerry. The expression on his face was sympathetic, but he wasn't stupid enough to say what he thought.

'Why don't you run on home to Mummy?' cooed Steve sarcastically.

'Your old man will kiss it better,' smirked Dean.

'I'm all right,' I said.

'I suppose you want a game too,' said Neil.

'Sure,' I said, struggling to disguise a sob. 'I'll play.'

'Is he any good?' asked Steve.

'Not bad at all,' said Neil. 'But not in the same class as Gerry. He hasn't got the bottle.'

I was relieved to find myself on Gerry's side. The game that followed was really bruising. Gerry took an elbow in the face when he was about to score, and I had to pick myself up more than once after a crunching tackle.

'You and your game of footy,' I grumbled to Gerry after yet another jarring challenge.

'Just play, will you?' growled Gerry.

But we didn't. Steve Delaney suddenly declared the game over.

'There's one of them now!' he bellowed, racing for the railings. 'That's Danny Skinner.'

The moment Danny saw Steve, he made a run for it. I dare say he'd been battling since he could walk and he could smell danger a mile off.

'Get him!' yelled Dean.

'Cut him off,' ordered Steve as Danny made for an alley that led to his back gate.

Dean reached the bollards before Danny and barred the way.

'I've got a message for your Graham,' spat Steve.

'Yes,' said Danny, doing his best to sound unconcerned. 'What's that?'

Steve grined maliciously. 'This.'

Without warning he butted Danny in the face. Danny sank to his knees, blood spilling from his nose. It was so unfair. Danny was only my age. Why didn't Steve pick on somebody his own size?

'Tell him to name the time and place,' said Steve. 'Him and his gang are going to get their heads kicked in for coming down our end of the estate last night.'

'You're the one who'll get his head kicked in,' cried Danny defiantly, earning a ferocious kick in the ribs from Dean. 'Our Graham will eat you alive.'

'You reckon?' said Steve, standing over his victim.

He yanked Danny to his feet and cuffed him round the ear. 'I don't think so, son, I don't think so.'

'On your way Skinner,' ordered Dean. 'And don't forget to pass on the message.'

I wasn't around to see what happened next. The church clock had just chimed nine o'clock. Even if I ran all the way home, I knew I was going to get my ear bent. My mum had probably sent the old man out to look for me already.

'Gerry,' I shouted. 'I've got to get off home. Are you coming?'

Gerry shook his head. As I ran off I glanced back. He and Neil were laughing and joking.

FIVE

Followed

W HAT DO YOU THINK?' DAD ASKED, WIPING HIS HANDS
'It looks wonky,' I told him.

'It is not wonky,' Dad insisted. 'I'm using a spirit level. What am I using?'

'You're using a spirit level, Dad.'

'That's right,' said Dad, 'And do you know what that means?'

'You're measuring ghosts?'

'It means,' said Dad, 'that this barbecue is straight and level.'

'What about this bit?' I asked pointing to one brick that was about as straight and level as a Chicago gangster.

'That?' said Dad. 'It looks all right to me.'

'If you say so.'

'I do,' said Dad. 'We'll have a barbecue when it's finished. Why don't you invite Gerry round?'

'Something up, John?' asked Dad.

'Dunno.'

'I do.' said Dad. 'You've got a face like a yard of pump water.'

'It's Gerry,' I told him.

'What about Gerry?'

'He's started hanging round with the Delaneys.'

'Oh,' said Dad. 'That shower. So what are you going to do about it?'

'Do?'

'Well,' said Dad, 'he is your best mate. If he's got any sense he'll soon forget about the Delaneys.'

'I'll go round now,' I said.

'Oh, John,' said Dad, as I walked down the path.

'Yes?'

'If he is hanging round with those idiots, you come straight home. OK?'

'Sure Dad,' I said. 'I'm not soft.'

Dad winked and turned back to his barbecue. I smiled to myself. It was definitely wonky.

'Oh,' said Gerry. 'It's you.'

'Don't sound so glad to see me,' I said.

'What do you want?'

'Funny question for a mate.'

'You'd better come in,' said Gerry.

I followed him into the living-room. His dad was there watching an Australian soap.

'Who's that?' called Mrs McEvilly from upstairs.

'Only John,' said Gerry.

'Do you want to go somewhere?' I asked.

'Like where?' asked Gerry.

'Anywhere.'

'Tell you what,' said Gerry. 'I'll bring a ball. We'll have a game of attack and defence in the Sally Army car park.'

'Why there?' I asked suspiciously. It was too close to Bride Lane for my liking.

'Why not?' asked Gerry.

'We're going out,' Gerry shouted.

Nobody answered.

'Hang on,' I said. 'What's happened to your video?'

'You noticed then?' said Gerry.

'Yes,' I said. 'I knew there was something last time I was round. It's just come to me. The telly's different too, isn't it?'

Gerry kicked the ball along the pavement. 'We got burgled last week.'

'You never!'

'Yes, they kicked the back door in when we were at the Strand.'

'Did they take much?' I asked.

'Electrical stuff. The TV and video, CD player, my Sega, the microwave.'

'When do you get the insurance money?' I asked.

'There is no insurance money,' said Gerry.

'What?'

'You heard,' he said. 'Dad had stopped paying it. He said we couldn't afford to keep it up.'

'So how do you get your things back?'

'We don't,' said Gerry glumly. 'My gran gave us that portable telly. We can kiss the rest goodbye.'

'That's terrible,' I said.

'Anyway,' he asked as we reached the Sally Army. 'Who's attacking?'

'Go on,' I said. 'You go first.'

I was doing my best to block him when I heard footsteps.

'Don't look now,' I warned Gerry. 'But we've got visitors.

It was Danny Skinner and his mates. They were at the end of the road. The moment they saw us they started yelling.

'That's all we need,' said Gerry.'

'Well,' I asked. 'What now?'

'Hey, McEvilly!' shouted Danny, 'I want a word with you.'

'Let's make a break for it, Ger,' I suggested.

'No,' said Gerry, eyeing the advancing gang. 'We'll be all right. Just follow me. Steve will sort them out.'

'Steve?' I repeated. 'What's he got to do with anything?'

'Didn't I tell you?' asked Gerry. 'I was going to see the gang after our kick around.'

'Why didn't you let on?' I demanded, aware that Danny had broken into a run.

'Would you have come?' asked Gerry

'Of course not.'

'That's why I didn't tell you.'

'Here they come,' I warned, as we passed the old shoe factory.

'I know,' said Gerry. 'Let's just hope the boys are on time.'

'Since when were you so pally with the Delaneys?' I asked.

Gerry didn't answer.

'You've joined the gang, haven't you?' I asked.

'So what if I have?'

'This is stupid,' I said, hearing the Bride Lane kids' footsteps getting closer. 'I don't know why I came with you.'

'Neither do I,' said Gerry. 'All you do is winge. You've got no bottle.'

'Oh, come on Ger. Let's leg it.'

'Run if you want,' he answered. 'I'll pick my own time.'

'You're not going anywhere, McEvilly,' came Danny Skinner's voice behind us. *If there's anybody up there*, I prayed silently, get me out of here.

'Who's going to stop me?' asked Gerry.

My heart was banging in my chest. What was Gerry doing? The odds were against us. Six onto two. *Oh please, just beam me up, Scotty.*

'Let's have a little word about last night,' said Danny. His face still showed the bruising from the beating he had taken, and he was in a nasty mood.

'Look Danny,' I croaked. 'We don't want any trouble.'

'Shut it,' ordered Danny. 'I'm talking to the organ grinder, not the monkey.'

'Run for it!' shrieked Gerry. Oh great, *now* he makes a break for it! He was already on his toes, heading for the cemetery wall.

'Get them!' yelled Danny.

Gerry was leaving the Bride Lane kids behind, but that was no consolation to me. I was so scared I was running as though my legs were tied together. They were catching up on me, and fast.

'Come on!' Gerry urged, as he scrambled over the wall. 'Move yourself.'

'I can't!' I yelled helplessly. I was being sandwiched by Danny and another boy.

'Right you,' snapped Danny, swinging me round by the jacket sleve. 'You're coming with us.'

'No way,' I cried, struggling to get free.

As the gang pinned my arms I could see Gerry making his getaway. He was already out of the cemetery and running across the main road towards the flyover.

'I'll get you McEvilly,' shouted Danny. 'I'll find out where you live.'

Danny turned to me. 'And you're the one to tell me.'

'I don't know,' I said.

'Don't give me that,' said Danny. 'You're his mate. We can always make you take a lie-detector test.'

'Lie-detector, what lie-detector?'

'Him,' said Danny, pointing to a fat kid who looked like somebody had screwed his head on the wrong way. 'Tell him a lie and he'll rip your arm off. Now, where will I find Gerry McEvilly?'

I looked away.

'Come on,' said Danny threateningly. 'You're going to show us.'

'My legs were turning to jelly. Gerry was right; I didn't

have any bottle. I turned reluctantly towards Gerry's, wondering how I was going to get out of this one.

'Uh oh,' said one of the other lads suddenly.

I followed the direction he was looking in. Approaching across waste land were eight or nine of the English Martyrs. Gerry hadn't abandoned me; he'd gone for reinforcements.

'Don't just stand there,' Danny shouted. 'Run!'

Even a tough nut like Danny knew when he was outnumbered,

'We'll see you again,' the lie-detector snapped, shoving me roughly to the ground before making his escape.

'See them run!' gloated Neil as he sprinted past me.

'Are you all right?' asked Gerry.

'Yes,' I answered, nursing a sore knee. 'No thanks to you.'

'You'd have been all right if you'd kept running,' said Gerry. 'Why did you slow down? Were you scared?'

'Does Bugs Bunny eat carrots?'

'Well,' said Gerry. 'If you want to be in the gang you'd better toughen up. Don't get scared, get even.'

I knew the tough talk was all show, but I didn't see the point of arguing with Gerry when the gang were around.

'That's just it,' I told him. 'I don't want to be in your stupid gang.'

SIX

Just like Danny

G ERRY AND I HAD HARDLY SPOKEN AT SCHOOL, SO IT came as a bit of a surprise when he called for me that evening.

'Coming out?' he asked as if we'd never exchanged a cross word.

'What about the gang?

'What about them?'

'I'm not coming out if you're going with them.'

'Fair enough,' said Gerry. 'Just us.'

'Something up?' I asked, noticing how unhappy he looked.

'Just the usual,' said Gerry. 'I can't weigh my dad up. We had this big heart-to-heart tonight about how he'd been a bit fed up but he was going to make an effort not to shout at me all the time. Ten minutes later he was chasing me round the house trying to land me one.'

'What for?'

'All I did was mend my bike in the back kitchen.'

I smiled.

'OK, so maybe I was wrong, but you should have seen

him. One minute he's all smiles, the next he's going to knock my block off.'

'Sounds like somebody else I know.'

'Meaning?'

'Think about it, Gerry.'

We hung around the chippy for a while with some of the kids from the Martyrs then took a slow walk up to Gerry's. There isn't much to do on North City at the best of times. In fact, watching the traffic lights change is a big night out round here.

'Isn't that your dad?' I asked, as we came round the back way.

'Has he got an armchair stuck to his behind?' asked Gerry.

'No.'

'Then it can't be him.'

'It is you know.'

Gerry's dad was at his back gate, peering along the brook.

'What's he doing?' I wondered aloud.

'If he's got off his backside,' Gerry grumbled. 'It can only be one thing.'

'What's that?'

'Somebody's nicked the telly.'

'No, look.'

Gerry's dad suddenly burst from his garden and pounced on somebody. A moment later who should appear, kicking and struggling from behind a bush, but Danny Skinner.

'What *is* going on?' I asked.

'Stay here,' said Gerry. 'I don't want Danny knowing this is where I live.' So we watched from a short distance.

'Danny's had it for sure,' whispered Gerry. 'Dad's in one of his moods.'

'What do you think you're doing, lad?' shouted Gerry's dad. 'Come on, what have you been up to?'

'I didn't do anything.' Danny's face was twisted in a resentful scowl, but he looked as scared as he was angry.

Gerry's dad jerked a thumb in the direction of his neighbour's garden.

'Don't give me that. I saw you and another boy in there.'

'No, you never.'

Gerry's dad tightened his grip on Danny's collar.

'Breaking into the garden shed, is that it?'

Danny's silence spoke volumes.

'Somebody ought to knock some sense into you,' Gerry's dad went on. 'They haven't got much money. You're hurting your own, that's what you're doing.' Danny just stared down at the ground.

'Oh, I give up,' sighed Gerry's dad. 'Get out of my sight.'

'I like that,' said Gerry. 'He never lets me off.'

Danny gave a defiant smirk and started to jog away. He'd hardly gone more than a few paces when a burly, red-haired man came panting along the side of the brook towards him.

'Hey you!' he barked.

Danny froze.

'Yes you.'

I recognized the red-haired man. He was Gerry's neighbour.

'Are you the one who broke the lock off my shed?'

Danny tried to run but the man seized his arm roughly.

'I've been all over the back field looking for you. Now, this is what you get for trying to rob me.'

He clenched a fist ready to strike.

'No!'

Gerry's dad stepped between them.

'You've got the wrong boy,' he said.

'He looks like the one to me,' the man said doubtfully.

'No honestly,' said Gerry's dad. 'I saw the whole thing from the kitchen window. The boy who did it ran off towards the main road.'

The red-haired man frowned then slowly relaxed his grip.

'Are you quite sure, Barry?'

Gerry's dad forced a smile. 'Positive.'

'Lucky for you Mr McEvilly was around,' said the neighbour. 'Now beat it.' Danny couldn't believe his luck. Pausing only to dart a puzzled glance at Gerry's dad he made good his escape.

Standing next to me, Gerry was staring at his father with a strange expression on his face.

'I don't believe it,' he said as we emerged from behind the bush.

'Why did you stand up for Danny?' I asked Mr McEvilly.

'Danny,' said Gerry's dad. 'Is that his name?'

'Yes,' I told him. 'he's one of the Skinners.'

'Whoever he is,' said Gerry's dad, 'I couldn't see that thumping him would do much good.'

'Typical!' cried Gerry.

His father turned and stared.

'I get a few spots of oil on the floor,' Gerry yelled, 'And you go mad at me. But when it comes to Danny rotten Skinner . . .'

His voice choked off.

'Gerry,' said his dad. 'Don't you see? I expect better from you. That's why I get so upset when you . . .'

Gerry wasn't listening. He turned and ran off across the field.

I caught up with him by the derelict garages on the far side.

'Is he still there?' asked Gerry.

'Your dad, yes he's watching us.'

'Good,' said Gerry. Without a moment's hesitation he picked up a bottle and hurled it against the garage wall.

'There,' said Gerry as it smashed. 'Now I'm just like Danny Skinner.'

SEVEN

The story of a Beefburger

PHIL SMITH WAS THE FIRST TO NOTICE IT. 'HAVE YOU read the menu?' he asked breathlessly.

'No,' I answered. 'Why?'

'Just take a look.'

'Who did that?' I asked.

'Beats me,' said Phil. 'Hey, Andy, Chris, take a look at this.'

As my classmates crowded round the menu board, I read it a second time. There in black and white it read *Bluebottle on a bun*. We knew what it was meant to be, of course. We had it the same day every week. It was supposed to read *Beefburger*, but instead, in bold capital letters it read *Bluebottle on a bun*. Soon there was a crowd of maybe twenty kids around the board.

'What's going on here?' boomed a familiar voice.

The crowd melted away as if by magic, leaving half a dozen of us who were still waiting to be served. The reason for the panic was the appearance of Mr Doyle, the head.

'Well?' he asked. 'There must be something very interesting for lunch today. What is it?'

Phil and I edged away. We didn't want to be in the firing

line when Mr Doyle read the offending phrase. In the event, he didn't say a word. He merely took a damp cloth from one of the dinner ladies and rubbed the board clean.

'Get on with your dinners,' he said, noticing dozens of pairs of eyes trained on him.

As he swept towards his office Phil gave a low whistle. 'I thought he'd go berserk,' he remarked.

'He would if somebody did it again,' said a voice behind us.

It was Neil Delaney, and for some reason he was staring pointedly at Gerry. We'd hardly spoken since the weekend and I was a bit put out to discover him in Neil's company.

'Go on, Ger,' urged Neil, producing a stick of chalk. 'Nobody's looking.'

Gerry's face went white.

'Not scared, are you?' sneered Neil.

Gerry looked around. Satisfied that the teachers and dinner ladies were busy, he crept over to the board. He thought for a moment or two then wrote in his spidery scrawl *Beefbangers make you burp*. I couldn't believe my eyes. Gerry used to do just about anything to keep out of trouble and here he was tweaking the tiger's tail.

'Yes?'

I looked up. Mrs McCartney the head dinner lady was tapping her ladle against an aluminium tray full to the brim with curry sauce. 'Burger on a bun or curry?' she asked.

'I don't know.' I was still staring at Gerry's handiwork.

Mrs McCartney's eyes followed mine. 'The cheeky little hounds!' she exclaimed. 'They've done it again.'

'Done what?' asked Neil innocently.

'You know what,' said Mrs McCartney. 'Did you do it?' she snapped, glaring at me. 'You look dead shifty, you do.'

'No,' I answered. 'Honest.'

She leaned across the counter. 'Mrs King, could I have a word?'

Our class teacher was stapling work to one of the display boards.

'Yes, what is it?' she asked pleasantly.

'That,' said Mrs McCartney. 'They've been messing with the board again. And Mr Doyle has rubbed it off once.'

At the mention of Mr Doyle's name, the smile vanished from Mrs King's face.

'I'll tell Mr Doyle,' she said. 'Keep these children here.'

As Mrs King went off in search of him, Mrs McCartney stood hands on hips, swinging a ladle threateningly and glaring at us as if we'd just mugged a nun. 'One of you has had it now,' she warned.

'Have you lost your marbles?' I asked Gerry.

'Shut up you!' he shot back irritably. I think he was getting worried.

'How do we get out of this one?' I demanded, ignoring him.

'Just keep your trap shut, Ryan,' Neil ordered, his eyes narrowing.

I didn't need telling twice. It was a case of shut your trap before I shut it for you. Just then Mrs King returned with Doyley.

'It was them lads,' said Mrs McCartney. 'I reckon it was that one.'

She was pointing straight at me.

'Now, now, Mrs McCartney,' said Doyley. 'You can't go accusing people without proof.'

I felt something, like a hand tugging at my trouser pocket. Neil reminding me to keep my mouth shut, no doubt.

'I think we'd better go to my office,' Doyley continued.

As we trooped from the hall the whole school was completely silent.

'I don't suppose anyone would care to own up,' he said, closing the door.

He supposed right. Everyone just stood shuffling their feet or staring fixedly at the carpet.

'Then you'd better empty your pockets,' he sighed.

He must have spotted the confused looks because he immediately added: 'I assume one of you still has the chalk.'

I couldn't avoid stealing a glance at Gerry. He was for it now.

'You first Neil,' said Doyley as pointedly as he could. Neil duly laid his belongings on the table.

Thirteen pence, a greyish handkerchief and two crumpled crisp packets.

'Thomas.'

A rubber dimetrodon, three pence and an oak leaf.

'Julie.'

'I haven't got pockets, Mr Doyle.'

Doyley smiled. 'Fair enough. Gerry.'

I took a deep breath, but to my surprise there was no stick of chalk among his belongings. His eyes met mine for a second.

'John T.'

John T. was John Turner from Class 11. There were so many Johns in school that everyone was known by the first letter of their surname. Still no chalk. Just a marble, three paper clips and a creased Everton programme.

'John R.' I dug a hand into my pocket and gasped.

'Is there something wrong?' asked Doyley.

'No,' I said. 'I mean . . .'

What *did* I mean? How could I explain it? There, smooth and dangerous at my fingertips was the incriminating stick of chalk. Doyley said no more. Instead he raised an inquiring eyebrow.

As I placed the chalk on his desk I attempted an explanation. 'I don't know how it got there, honest Mr Doyle.'

'The rest of you may get your lunch,' said Doyley cooly.

It was with dumb helplessness that I watched the other kids filing out. I suddenly understood Neil's sly prod. As the door closed, Doyley sat behind his desk.

'OK John,' he said, 'Let's hear what you've got to say for yourself, son.'

'Cheers, Gerry.' My voice was thick with sarcasm.

Gerry half turned. He looked embarrassed. 'Come again?'

'I said thanks – thanks for nothing.'

'What are you on about Ryan?'

Ryan! We really had fallen out this time.

'I'm on about what you did in there.'

'I didn't do anything.'

I shook my head. 'No, maybe you didn't, but you know who did.'

'Meaning?'

'Meaning somebody planted that chalk on me.'

Gerry glanced over his shoulder. 'Have you seen Neil around?'

'Yes, he's over there taxing that second year.'

We watched Neil walking across the yard munching the poor kid's crisps.

'It was Neil,' Gerry confided. 'He took the chalk off me.'

'I thought it must have been,' I said. 'You're one brain-dead divvy, but I knew you couldn't stoop that low.'

'No?' asked Gerry, looking really miserable.

'Why didn't you speak up for me?' I demanded, too angry to be silenced by a half-hearted threat like that.

'What, and fall out with Neil and the boys? I don't want them ganging up on me. Do I look stupid?'

'You must be to hang around with Delaneys.'

'Oh, think what you like,' he said. 'I'm off.'

'Not so fast,' I said. 'I want you to put it right. You're going to tell Doyley what really happened.'

'Oh, am I?'

'I thought you were my mate.'

'Why should I tell on Neil, anyway? Doyley will soon forget about it.'

'Of course he will, but not until after the Inter-School semis.'

Gerry frowned. 'What's that got to do with anything?'

'He's dropped me from the team,' I yelled. 'Doyley's kicked me out of the team for what happened in the hall.'

'For good?'

'No, just for the one match but that's not the point. If I miss the semi I won't stand much of a chance of playing in the final, will I?'

'You'll play,' said Gerry. 'Phil's no threat.'

'But he doesn't scrawl on the menu board,' I cried.

'Doyley might go over the top once in a while,' Gerry said 'but he isn't going to keep punishing you for a little thing like that. He'll want his best team out for that big game with the posh school'

Though we were still two games away from it, everybody was talking about this new event in the football calendar. Whoever won the Liverpool Inter-Schools Trophy would qualify to play the area's top public school in a two leg friendly.

'Well,' I complained bitterly. 'If we do get through I could still miss it the way things are going. You've got to do the right thing. It's up to you now.'

'What is?'

My heart sank. Unnoticed by either of us, Neil had come over to see why we were arguing.

'Well, I'm listening,' he snarled. 'What's going on?'

'Nothing, Neil,' Gerry answered. 'Honest.'

Neil wasn't impressed. 'If either of you are thinking of blabbing to Doyley, forget it. Understood?'

'Lighten up, Neil,' said Gerry, mustering a thin smile. 'Who said anything about grassing you up to Doyley?'

'Don't take me for an idiot,' warned Neil. 'I know what's going on.'

As he turned to walk away I grabbed his sleeve. I still don't know what made me do it, but grab him I did.

'Got a death wish, Ryan?' Neil asked, peeling my fingers from his jacket.

'Calm down, John,' cried Gerry. 'He'll batter you.'

'I'd listen to Gerry if I were you,' said Neil, poking me in the chest.

The anger which had swept through me was ebbing as quickly as it had risen. I hung my head.

'Are you going to say anything?' he asked.

'No,' I murmured.

'Louder,' he insisted. 'Are you going to grass me up?'

'No, Neil,' I repeated. 'I won't say a word.'

'Good.' His face was a picture of smug satisfaction. 'Now, what about you Gerry, are you still with the gang?'

Gerry gave me a sideways glance.

'Well?'

'Yes.' He followed Neil across the yard. 'I'm still with the gang.'

EIGHT

The big nothing

'D ROPPED!'
'That's right,' I said. 'And I didn't do it either.'

'I hope you told Mr Doyle that,' said Dad.

I watched him mixing the mortar. The barbecue was nearly finished.

'You did tell him, didn't you?' asked Dad.

'Not exactly.'

'You're not covering up for somebody, I hope.'

My silence said everything.

'You are, aren't you? Who is it? Not Gerry?'

I lowered my eyes. 'Sort of. He wrote it, but it was Neil who planted the chalk.'

Dad frowned at the mention of Neil Delaney. 'You're not hanging around with him, are you?'

'Of course not!'

Mum relieved a tense situation by letting the twins into the garden.

'Can the girls watch?' she asked. 'Go on babes, watch Daddy playing with the bricks.'

'Silly Daddy,' said Rachel.

Dad smiled. 'Anyway,' he said, turning his attention to

me. 'What are you going to do?'

'What can I do?'

'You can speak to Gerry.'

'I tried, remember.'

'Then try again,' said Dad. 'Friendships are like this barbecue of mine. They can take a few knocks.'

As if to prove his point he gave the barbecue a gentle shove. The whole lot came crashing down.

'Thanks Dad,' I said. 'That makes me feel much better.'

As I turned the corner into Gerry's road I saw Kieran and Susie sitting on the front path playing with coloured chalks.

'Is Gerry in?' I asked.

'No,' said Kieran. 'He went out with some big boys.'

I felt a pang of unease.

'Do you know who they were?' I asked.

Kieran shook his head. It was a stupid question to ask a five-year-old.

'Which way did they go?'

Kieran pointed in the direction of the boarded-up house across the road.

'Thanks,' I said.

I jogged along the back path and rejoined the road at the Sally Army, but there was no sign of Gerry.

'All right, John,' came a familiar voice. 'I didn't think you'd be coming.'

It was Tony Crawford from our class.

'I don't . . .'

'The big showdown,' Tony explained. 'It's tonight.'

'What big showdown?' I asked.

'Haven't you heard? Martyrs against Bride Lane. Winner takes all.'

'You're not going are you?' I asked.

'Of course I am,' said Tony. 'I wouldn't miss it for the world. We'll mince them.'

I couldn't believe my ears. First Gerry, now Tony. The gang seemed to be dragging them all in.

'Here are the boys now,' said Tony.

I turned to see the Delaneys and a crowd of kids. Right at the front walked Gerry.

'No sign of Bride Lane yet?' asked Neil.

Tony shook his head.

'They won't show,' said Dean. 'I told you they wouldn't.'

'They'll be here,' said Steve. 'We're on their turf.'

Gerry was looking at me. 'What are you doing here?'

'I might ask you the same question,' I retorted.

'Are you staying?' he asked.

I shook my head. 'What, and get my head kicked in?'

With that, I set off home. I was still in earshot of the gang when I heard the long, shrill blast of a referee's whistle. At the signal kids came running from the opposite end of the car park. They outnumbered the Martyrs and they'd taken out two or three of them before anybody really realised what was happening.

'Right,' bawled Danny Skinner. 'Where's Steve Delaney?'

I could only see Neil. He was rolling on the ground with another boy and he was taking a hammering as his opponent slammed his fist repeatedly into Neil's face. As for Steve, he'd already taken to his heels.

'I don't believe it,' I gasped out loud. 'He's running away.'

There he was, scuttling away like a frightened rabbit.

Steve and Dean were scaling the high spiked railings which bordered the cemetery, abandoning the other gang members to their fate. They didn't get far. Graham Skinner appeared with two other former Bride Lane boys and dragged them off the railings.

'Are you the one who's been shooting his mouth off about me?' he roared into Steve's face.

'Drop dead,' was Steve's reply. He must have been at the back of the queue when they handed out the tact.

Graham's eyes narrowed, then he butted Steve over the left eye. His fist came up a split-second later and jabbed into Steve's chest.

'Going to take me, are you?' he mocked. 'On my own turf?'

Steve raised a hand to his cheek, but I think it was his pride that was really bruised.

'Hey, Danny,' he shouted. 'Are these the two that did you over?'

Danny nodded, a twinkle in his eyes.

'Right,' Graham announced. 'You've had it.'

He pinned Steve's arms, while two others grappled Dean to the ground.

'Beg,' he ordered.

Steve didn't answer.

'I said beg!'

Graham accompanied the word with a sharp kick in the ribs. That did it. Steve's nerve broke. He began to babble so fast I couldn't make out the words. It was only then, watching the leaders of the gang pleading miserably that I remembered Gerry. I looked around, scanning the car park, the streets and entries.

'Get out of here quick,' came a voice.

It was Tony Crawford. He'd managed to wriggle free of his opponent while Dean and Steve surrendered. 'They'll be after us next.'

I took the hint and followed him over a garden fence. We ran down an entry and into Windsor Close. From there it was possible to cut across the old playing field onto the allottments.

'Did you see where Gerry went?' I panted.

'Gerry McEvilly? No, I haven't seen him since it started. If he had any sense he'd have run off when Bride

Lane made an appearance. We weren't in their league; it was a walk-over.'

'Did you get hit?' I asked.

'Not half,' said Tony. 'This fat kid jumped me before I knew what was happening. He was bashing my head on the playground. Look.' He displayed a crimson patch around the eye.

'You're going to have a shiner tomorrow,' I said.

'Two if my mum knows what I've been doing,' he murmured.

'Bad news, wasn't it?' I asked.

'Yes, I never thought Steve would beg like that. What a moron.'

'You wouldn't say that to his face,' I told him.

'Why shouldn't I after tonight? I used to think he was really something. Some hero!'

'Just imagine if we had to play Bride Lane next,' I said.

'Don't even think about it,' said Tony ruefully.

'See you Tony.' I said, as we reached the end of his road.

I trudged home watching the sun setting behind the row of red-brick houses. As I remembered Steve begging at Graham Skinner's feet I couldn't help feeling a touch of satisfaction.

NINE

Supersub

I DROPPED GRATEFULLY TO THE GROUND. GOOF HAD worked us hard that Thursday night. He was mad about stamina training. I just wished he'd put a bit of trust in natural talent. It wouldn't half make life easier.

'I suppose you'll be wanting to know who's in the team?' he said.

I grimaced. Of all the teams in the whole city it had to be Bride Lane in the final. Death or glory, Gerry said. If we won we'd be the kings of the North End. If we lost our lives wouldn't be worth living. Death or glory. Maybe it would be better if I stayed dropped. I stole a glance at the other lads. No, I was bound to be picked. Sure, Phil Smith had run his socks off as sub, but nobody really rated him. One full game for the team didn't make him a serious contender.

Goof fumbled in his grip for the clipboard that held the team selection.

'Here we are, lads, Now listen up, I'm only going to read this once. Some of us have got homes to go to, you know.'

He reeled off the names starting with Richie Harris in

goal. He was always picked if only because nobody else wanted to play in goal. One by one the team members either smiled or gave a cursory nod. They were in, I tugged the grass anxiously. Suddenly, I didn't care whether we were playing Bride Lane or Werewolves Athletic. I had to play, I just had to.

Come on, Goof, let's have the front four.

Gerry would be in, of course, he was an automatic selection. Then there was Neil, who got picked for his height and his aggression. Tony Crawford was another cert. He could nearly match Gerry for speed and he had a good left foot.

That left one place. It was between Phil and me. I stared at him. Phil? Surely not? He was slow and had the positional sense of a blindfolded slug.

'Tony Crawford, Neil Delaney – and keep it clean, Neil. I don't want you getting sent off in the final.'

Neil just grinned proudly. Somehow his reputation had survived the fiasco at Bride Lane.

'Gerry McEvilly and . . .' Goof looked up from the clipboard.

I couldn't believe it; his eyes were on Phil. ' . . . Phil Smith. Well done, Supersub.'

Supersub! Twenty minutes hard running against Greenway and he was getting picked ahead of me. It was so unfair, I'd been an ever-present member of the team until I got dropped for that nonsense over the beefburger.

'You're sub for the final, John. Sorry son, but Phil had a good game against Greenway.'

Phil was beaming. This was awful, the kid was a nerd. To him, football was just a hobby. I belonged to the Bill Shankly school: Football isn't a matter of life and death; it's more important than that!

'Hard luck, Ryan,' said Neil as I trudged off the field. His hand was on my shoulder, his way of reminding me to keep my mouth shut about the chalk. 'I'm sure you'll get a game.'

'No thanks to you.' I remarked.

His fingers pressed into my upper arm. 'Don't push it, Ryan.'

'Get your hands off me, Neil,' I snapped, shoving him off.

'Hey, hey, what's all this?' It was Goof.

'Nothing,' Neil replied quickly. 'Just mucking about.'

He gave me a warning look, but I didn't need it. I wasn't about to blow him up to Goof.

'Sure?' asked Goof.

'Yes, no problem Mr Scarry,' I assured him. I watched him ambling awkwardly away as if he'd left the coat hangers in his clothes. Whoever nick-named him Goofy deserved a medal. It had him down to a tee. I swung my bag over my shoulder ready to go.

'You did well there, Ryan,' said Neil. 'Just keep your mouth shut and you'll be all right. Are you listening to me?'

I just gave him a look of utter hatred and tried to push past.

'I said, are you listening to me?'

At that moment I'd had enough of listening to Neil Delaney. Drawing back my fist I punched him right on the nose.

I'd like to say he fell screaming to the ground, but he hardly flinched.

'You,' he said, grinding his teeth. 'You're dead.'

Without another word Neil hurled himself at me. As I slipped and fell he jumped on top of me.

'Fight!' yelled Tony Crawford. 'It's Neil and John.'

In fact, it wasn't much of a fight. I was writhing and struggling while Neil sat astride me raining the blows into my face and chest.

'Get off!' I screamed. 'Get off!'

He hit me again and again, but it wasn't the punches which hurt most. It was the humiliation. I wasn't even able to fight back. He had my shoulders pinned to the ground and was able to do just what he liked.

It was just how I'd felt as Gerry was being drawn into the gang, the same sense of utter helplessness and failure.

'Get off!'

There was grass in my mouth and my tears were mixed with soil from the field.

'Get off!'

Through my tears I could see Gerry staring down at me. *What are you looking at?* I thought. *You got me into this.*

'Nobody talks to me the way you did,' shrieked Neil, beside himself with fury.

Suddenly, as quickly as the onslaught had begun, it ended. Spitting out grass and soil, I sat up groggily. To my surprise I saw Neil and Gerry squaring up to each other.

'What are you doing Ger?' demanded Neil. 'Why did you pull me off him?'

Gerry didn't say a word.

'You're a gang member,' said Neil, 'You take a gang member's side. Always.'

Still not a word from Gerry.

'Is there something wrong, Ger?' Neil persisted.

'Yes,' Gerry answered quietly, 'You.'

'You what?'

'Oh, listen Neil. I just want you to leave John alone, that's all.'

Gerry started to help me up while Neil looked on.

'Are you OK?' asked Gerry.

'I think so,' I said.

'Have you gone crackers?' asked Neil.

'No,' said Gerry. 'I think I'm just coming to my senses.'

Giving up Gerry as a bad job, Neil made a bee-line for Tony Crawford, but Tony saw him coming and ran to his dad who had come to pick him up.

'He's a bit short of friends all of a sudden isn't he?' said Phil.

'It's no wonder,' I said, wincing at the discomfort of a swollen lip.

'Come on, lads' said Gerry. 'Let's have a walk around the park lake on the way home.'

'No can do,' said Phil. 'My dad's waiting too. He's taking me to ju-jitsu.'

Gerry and I watched him slide into the front seat of his dad's new Rover.

'The boy who has everything,' said Gerry. His parents didn't even have a car, never mind anything as flash as an August registered Rover.

'Including my place in the team,' I added.

'Yes, that was a bit off,' remarked Gerry.

'You reckon?'

'Of course I do, you're miles better than Phil.'

'It looks like I'm still paying for that stupid trick with the chalk.'

Gerry shook his head. 'We could do with you against Bride Lane. They'll clog Phil out of the game.'

'I'm not so good at the rough stuff either, you know.'

Gerry grinned. 'Against a headcase like Neil,' he said, 'who is?'

It was my turn to smile,

'You didn't do too badly,' I said. 'How come you stuck up for me anyway?'

'I was sick with fright,' Gerry said, 'But I couldn't let him beat up my best mate, could I? We go back a long way. Feel up to a race?'

'Not really,' I replied. 'I'm still a bit sore.'

'Well, you'd better get fit,' said Gerry. 'We might still need you on Saturday.'

'I doubt it,' I said. 'Still, you can hope.'

'We'll never hear the last of it if we lose,' Gerry said.

That's when I asked him the question which had been forming in my mind ever since he pulled Neil off me.

'Gerry,' I began. 'Do you know what you did back there?'

Gerry's face clouded. 'How do you mean?'

'Well,' I explained. 'I don't think Neil's too happy.'

'I know,' said Gerry. He went very quiet. I think he was just beginning to realise the trouble he might be in.

We walked along the lakeside, asking the anglers how many they'd caught and cadging maggots.

'Dare you to put one in your mouth.' said Gerry.

'You what?'

'A maggot,' said Gerry. 'Try putting one in your cheek. It makes them wriggle and attract the fish. The old fellows do it. I've seen them.

'Disgusting,' I said.

Tossing our last maggots into the lake, we turned for home. It was on the path which led past the allotments that we heard a voice that made me feel worse than a whole mouthful of maggots. It belongd to Neil Delaney.

'Think you can leave the gang, do you McEvilly? Well, there's no way. If the Skinners don't get you first, we will. Me and our Steve will be seeing you soon.'

I glanced at Gerry, His face had drained of blood. He was scared – really scared.

TEN

Sudden death

'I DIDN'T THINK YOU'D BE BACK HERE IN A HURRY,' muttered Danny Skinner, as I passed the Bride Lane team.

I ignored him, pretending I hadn't heard.

'Well,' Danny called after me, 'you're on a hiding to nothing today. Don't you lot get sick of being battered?'

'Forget it,' Phil Smith advised in a hushed voice, 'They're just trying to wind us up.'

'Trying to wind *you* up,' I murmured. 'I'm not playing remember.'

Phil rolled his eys. 'Don't rub it in,' he complained. 'Goof picked the team, not me.'

Dad nodded across to Neil Delaney. 'I see he's still in the team,' he said. 'And all because of your stupid loyalty.'

I nodded absent-mindedly. I was hardly listening. The reason for my lack of interest was simple – Gerry hadn't shown. A thought flashed through my mind: what if the Delaneys had caught up with him? It was a thought I dismissed just as quickly. Neil was there in front of me, changed ready for the match. Whatever he had in store for Gerry, it wouldn't be until after the game.

'Has anybody seen Gerry McEvilly?' barked Goof irritably. Nobody had.

'What, not even you, John?'

'Not since last night, Mr Scarry.'

'It looks like you might get a game after all,' said Dad.

'Oh great,' I mumbled. 'Without Gerry it'll be a massacre.'

'Strip off,' Goof ordered. 'I can't wait for him any longer.'

'Hang on,' came a shut. 'Here he is now.'

Gerry's entrance was greeted with peals of laughter from Bride Lane.

'What's this, McEvilly?' Danny chuckled. 'Brought your fan club with you?'

Gerry scowled and made his way over to his teammates.

'What's with the shopping trolley?' asked Tony Crawford.

'What's with the kids might be a better question,' Goof added sourly. You could see he was annoyed. Not many players come to a football match pushing their brother and sister in a supermarket trolley.

'I couldn't help it, Mr Scarry,' Gerry panted. 'My mum said I'd got to take them with me. They got tired on the way.'

'So where did you get the trolley?' asked Goof suspiciously.

'I found it,' said Gerry, his mind working overtime. 'On . . . wasteland.'

'Mm.' Goof wasn't convinced. 'Anyway,' he said inspecting Susie and Kieran as if Gerry had arrived with a couple of ferrets, 'What happens to these two while you're playing?'

Both teams were on the pitch and the ref was eyeing his watch impatiently.

'They'll be ok,' said Gerry. 'Won't you kids?'

Kieran, the older one, nodded. Susie just sucked her thumb.

'No way, Gerry,' said Goof. 'They're too young to be left unsupervised. I don't know what your parents are thinking of, I really don't. Come on, John, you're on.'

I was dying to play, but not at Gerry's expense. If he didn't have his football, he didn't have anything.

'Dad,' I said.

'All right, son, all right.' Dad smiled and turned to Goof. 'I'll take responsibility for these two, Mr Scarry.'

'Are you quite sure, Mr Ryan?'

'Sure,' said Dad 'Go on, Gerry lad, play a blinder. Oh, and Gerry.'

'Yes, Mr Ryan?'

'Just remember what John's done for you. *Everything* he's done for you.'

'I will,' said Gerry, peeling off his track suit. 'Thanks. I owe you one.'

'Just beat Bride Lane,' I told him.

'I'm proud of you, son,' said Dad, as Gerry sprinted to the centre circle. 'I shouldn't have argued with you before. There's nothing wrong with loyalty. Poor Gerry. Barry couldn't even be bothered to come to watch him on his big day. I saw him the other day, you know.'

'Gerry's dad?'

'Yes, he said he didn't want to fall out with the lad. He told me he was worried about Gerry and all this gang stuff.'

'So why didn't he come today?'

'I don't know,' said Dad. 'He's been acting funny lately.'

'Just like Gerry,' I said, turning to watch the kick off. Bride Lane went straight onto the attack and kept up the pressure for most of the early stages. Whenever the Martyrs tried to counter attack they ran into this black kid called Gary Roberts. As defenders go, he made a great brick wall.

'Oh dear,' said Dad under his breath.

'Not doing too well, are we?' I asked.

'That's an understatement,' said Dad, feeding Kieran and Susie wine gums. 'The Martyrs are taking a hammering.'

'So what's new?' I sighed.

'This is better,' shouted Goof from the touchline as we finally crossed the centre line. 'Run it, Phil.'

'Bride Lane's attack had broken down on the left and Phil had picked up the loose ball. It was our first decent break.

'Go on, Phil,' his dad yelled. 'Take it all the way.'

'Cross it,' ordered Goof, clearly irritated by Mr Smith's interference. 'Cross it. Neil's free on this side.'

Goof was on a hiding to nothing. Phil was only ever going to take notice of one voice, his dad's. Pushing the ball into the penalty area, he tried to hurdle Gary Roberts' tackle.

'He tried to do too much,' Dad observed as Phil crashed heavily to the ground. 'He should have laid it off when he had the chance.'

Goof gave Phil's dad a stare, but Mr Smith ignored it. 'Get up, Phil,' he shouted. 'Get up. You're offside.'

Bride Lane picked up where they'd left off and pressed again. Danny wrong-footed Phil on the far touchline and powered down to the byeline. Richie came out, but Danny slipped it past him. I watched the ball rolling across the empty goal. Bride Lane's best striker was on hand and he was ready for it.

One – nil.

As Gerry passed me on his way down the field, I whispered to him. 'What's going wrong, Ger?'

'It's Neil,' he replied. 'His bottle's gone. It's because of that lot.' He was pointing at half a dozen Bride Lane scallies who were giving him a hard time whenever he got the ball. They were promising a repeat of the battering they'd just handed out to the Martyrs. It was mostly catcalls and gestures but it was doing the trick.

'Phil's no better. He's been a passenger since that tackle.'

The comment earned Gerry an offended glare from Phil's dad, but he was right. Phil was nursing a heavily-bruised shin and he was shying away from contested balls. The Martyrs had only half an attack.

'Come on, Gerry,' shouted Goof. 'Let's see some action.'

'I need support,' Gerry answered. 'Tony's the only one doing the business.'

Goof looked at his watch. 'Try to hold them till half-time. We'll have a word then.'

Gerry nodded, and shouted across to Neil. 'Come on, Neil lad, we need you.'

'Shut it, McEvilly,' said Neil, at the same time glancing uneasily at the Bride Lane kids. 'I don't need your advice.'

'Thank goodness for that,' said Dad as the half-time whistle blew. 'We're lucky not to be three down at least.'

'Well played, Richie,' said Goof. That said it all; the only praise went to our goalie! 'OK boys,' he continued. 'What do you call that?'

'Football,' said Phil.

'Really?' Goof responded. 'Well, I call it a disaster. A one-legged tortoise could do better. We're just lucky they've missed so many chances in front of goal. Listen Neil, if you don't pull your finger out, you're off. You've got to get into the game as well, Phil.'

Phil looked sheepishly towards his dad to see if he was listening, but Mr Smith was talking to one of the other parents, boasting about Phil's best run – Phil's *only* run.

'What I want to see,' said Goof, 'is some commitment. Got that? This is the final, lads. There's no second chance.'

Gerry sucked thoughtfully on a slice of orange. 'Why don't you bring John on?'

'I'll make the decisions,' snapped Goof. 'Now get out there and go after that equalizer like you mean it.'

The nods from the team were half-hearted. The lads had their heads down and Goof's pep talk was falling on deaf ears.

'Do it!' Goof barked as a parting shot.

I watched the team trooping back onto the field for the second half. 'What do you reckon, Dad?'

'I reckon the trophy's going to Bride Lane.' He hoisted Susie up onto his shoulders. 'That's your brother out there, babe,' he said. 'Cheer him on.'

Susie just sucked her thumb, but Kieran started yelling for Gerry at the top of his voice.

Straight from the kick off, Danny Skinner took the ball half the length of the field but Gerry tackled back like the terrier he was. To everybody's surprise the ref blew for a foul.

'Oh, come off it,' groaned Dad. 'The tackle was good.'

Good it may have been, but Bride Lane had a free kick on the edge of the penalty area. The ball was rolled to Danny. He met it with a ferocious drive that cannoned off the post.

'Our luck's in today, all right,' said Dad.

Gerry picked up the loose ball and set off down the pitch.

'Go on, Gerry,' I cried. 'Go on!'

He rode the first tackle then side-stepped a second.

'Like I said,' Dad commented with a wink. 'The boy's got the gift.'

When he beat Gary Roberts I thought he had the goal at his mercy, but I reckoned without Danny Skinner. He came pounding in from behind and flattened Gerry on the edge of the box.

'Penalty!' I exclaimed.

'Just outside,' said Dad. 'But he ought to be off for that.'

Neil thought so too. All his shame and frustration boiled

over and he flew at Danny, fists flailing. That was just what Danny had been waiting for. Drawing back his arm, he drove his fist into Neil's chest. Alerted by the reaction of the spectators, the ref turned towards them.

'It's all right,' said Goof, running onto the pitch and taking Neil by the elbow. 'A flash of temper. Neil here was to blame. I'm taking him off anyway.'

The ref nodded. 'That seems a very sensible decision Mr Scarry. This young man deserved to be sent off.'

Goof led Neil to the touchline and waved me to get on. 'Get changed Delaney. We'll talk about this in school on Monday.'

By the time I reached Gerry he was hobbling to his feet. 'Typical,' he grunted. 'Neil should have saved the aggro for his football then we might not be one down.'

Tony was standing over the ball, waiting for us to give him the nod. As I passed him I whispered to Gerry: 'Bend it, Ger.'

Tony glanced to his left and rolled the ball into Gerry's path. I knew the moment he struck it that it was goal-bound. As the ball shook the Bride Lane netting, Gerry raced over to the touchline, punching the air and winking at his brother and sister. Kieran was screaming fit to burst. Susie sucked her thumb.

'Nice one, Ger,' I said as we jogged back to the centre circle.

'Not really,' he said wrinkling his nose. 'I mis-hit it.'

'If that's a mis-cue,' I chuckled, 'I'd like to see it when you strike it cleanly.'

After the equalizer it was end-to-end stuff. The only thing that kept us from taking the lead was the tackling of Gary Roberts and Danny Skinner and a ref who wouldn't know a foul if it came up and broke his leg.

When the whistle blew for full-time, we flopped exhausted on the grass.

'I'm cream-crackered,' panted Gerry.

'Me too,' I said, gulping mouthfuls of air as if oxygen rationing began the next day. 'What now? Don't tell me it's extra time.'

'No,' said Gerry, 'penalty shoot out. If we're still even after five it's sudden death.'

I stole a glance at the Bride Lane kids. If we won, it might be just that! Tony Crawford took the first penalty. One – nil. Danny Skinner side-footed Bride Lane's equalizer. Both sides scored their second and third. Phil was up next. He placed the ball and took a few steps back. Bride Lane's goalie crouched, staring him out. Phil glanced nervously at his dad.

'Just hit it, will you?' ordered Gerry.

Phil began his run up, but he was so afraid of missing that he just couldn't concentrate. He seemed unsure whether to put it to the goalie's right or left. As it turned out he did neither, skying it over the crossbar. Well, that was it. The Bride Lane boys were on the pitch celebrating as if the trophy was already theirs.

As for Phil, he had his head down.

'Never mind, son,' said Mr Smith charitably. 'You did your best.'

When the ref had finally cleared the pitch, the shoot-out continued. Bride Lane scored again. 4 – 3.

'You next,' said Goof.

'Me?' I gasped. 'What about Gerry?'

Goof smiled. 'He's my secret weapon in case it goes to sudden death.'

I placed the ball and did my best not to see or hear anything except the ball and the goal. With my heart banging in my ribs I ran up and hit it. No placing, I just hit it.

'Goal!' sang Gerry jubilantly. 'Four all. Come on, Richie, you can save this one.'

Richie Harris stepped back into goal for the Martyrs. One of their defenders hit the ball for Bride Lane. It was low and hard, but too close to Richie who pounced on it gleefully.

'Good save!' said Goof. 'Now it's sudden death. Do the business, Gerry.'

Gerry only took two steps, then punted it into the bottom right hand corner of the goal. 5 – 4. The pressure was on Bride Lane now. Suddenly I was feeling cocky, if not downright suicidal. Turning to Bride Lane's supporters, I said loudly: 'Now let's see who's got bottle.'

As Bride Lane's last penalty-taker positioned the ball, Danny Skinner leaned forward. 'Miss it,' he warned, 'and you're dead.'

The boy took half-a-dozen steps, toe-poked the ball softly and watched in agony as it rolled harmlessly into Richie's arms.

'Brilliant!' shrieked Goof.

Nobody was arguing. We were.

Tony Crawford made a bee-line for Danny. 'Threatening your own player as he takes a penalty?' he taunted. 'Good tactics, Dan.'

Danny was furious, but there was nothing he could do about it. It was the Martyrs' day.

'What's happened to Neil?' asked Gerry, looking around.

'Why?' I asked. 'Are you worried about his threat?'

'I'd be stupid not to be,' said Gerry.

'He slunk away after the fight,' Dad told us. 'And what threat's this?'

Gerry and I exchanged guilty glances.

'Oh, nothing, Dad.'

ELEVEN

Doyley's idea

'*F*INALLY,' BOOMED DOYLEY AS HE ROCKED FROM HEEL to toe at the front of the assembly. 'I have to say a few words about our football team.'

Phil winked at me, Gerry just stared ahead. He'd been quiet all morning.

'Our older boys did us proud on Saturday afternoon,' Doyley continued. 'Many of you will probably know by now that the team won a keenly contested match in an exciting penalty shoot-out'

The news was greeted by grins, clenched fists and hisses of 'Yisss!'

'So,' said Doyley, raising his hands to restore order, 'Could I have the team out at the front of the hall please.'

Tony Crawford was the first up, followed by me and Richie Harris. Phil looked a bit embarrassed but he followed anyway. The others trailed up one by one, pretending to be modest but loving every minute of it. Gerry was still seated. Neil must have remained seated as well, but he'd been to Doyley's office to explain the sending off and I still couldn't see him.

'Come on Gerry,' said Doyley, 'You were our scorer and star player, after all.'

Gerry blushed bright red and shuffled to the front. That left only Neil still seated. I couldn't blame him. It was bad enough having a lousy game, but getting sent off as well! I scanned the rows of kids, but he wasn't there. I looked at Phil and Gerry, raising an eyebrow. Phil shrugged. Gerry stared at his shoes.

'Our victory in the Inter-Schools competition makes me especially proud. It's the first time we have won the trophy, and also means that we will now play one of the region's public schools. Our opponents are The Norton School in Greater Manchester. Gerry,' Doyley said, 'Would you collect the trophy from my office please?'

Gerry disappeared for a second before returning with the cup.

Doyley was beaming with pleasure. 'Let's show our appreciation of the team,' he said.

Everybody clapped for all they were worth. Doyley allowed the applause to continue until some of the third years started clapping rhythmically and a couple of the fourth year girls tried to start a Mexican wave.

'OK, OK,' said Doyley. 'That'll do, thank you very much.' The clapping subsided. 'Sit down, team,' he ordered, before carrying on in a more serious vein. 'I must however mention one incident of which I can't be proud. One of our boys and a member of the Bride Lane team fought on the pitch, and that is unforgivable.'

A murmur rippled through the assembly.

'So,' Doyley went on. 'I gave the matter some thought and approached the head teacher over at Bride Lane. I am aware that the fighting which occurred on Saturday wasn't the first incident between the two schools. It is for that reason, and in the light of the closeness of the result, that I made an offer.'

My mind was racing but I wasn't ready for what came next.

'I,' Doyley announced, 'have always believed that fair play is as important as winning, and I know that our team coach Mr Scarry agrees with me.'

Goof nodded vigorously from his seat at the side of the hall.

Doyley was at last getting to the point.

'When we travel to play at The Norton School this Wednesday five Bride Lane boys will be in our team.'

Well, you could have cut the atmosphere with a knife. Jaws dropped, mouths fell open, tongues hung out. Nobody could believe it. The Martyrs and their worst enemies together in the same team – it was unthinkable.

'The boys of both schools will be representing a joint North City Juniors team.'

I heard Doyley's words, but I just couldn't believe what he was saying. Did he really think everybody was going to let bygones be bygones and play as a team?

'The purpose of this cooperation,' Doyley summed up, 'is simple. The team will be representing not only their schools but their city. We will be playing boys from much more privileged backgrounds and we need to show what we're made of. Liverpool has its problems, but there's a lot of talent here too. I'm sure all the boys here and those from Bride Lane will make all of us proud.'

As we filed out I whispered to Gerry. 'What do you think of that?'

Gerry shook his head. 'Stupid, if you ask me.'

'Stop talking there,' shouted Mrs King. 'Oh, and John R . . .' All my classmates turned to stare. ' . . .could you go and see Mr Doyle before you come back to class?'

Now what?

'Off you go,' she repeated as I hesitated, holding up the whole line.

As I made my way to Doyley's office I was aware of everyone's eyes on my back.

'Come in,' he called when I knocked.

'Mrs King said you wanted to see me.'

'Yes, I do,' said Doyley. 'I had an interesting chat with Gerry McEvilly this morning just before school. Can you guess what we talked about?'

'The match?' I suggested.

'No, John, not football.' Doyley was smiling. That was a good sign at least. 'It concerned Neil Delaney. Now do you know what I'm talking about?'

'I think so,' I answered uncertainly.

'Gerry told me everything,' Doyley explained. 'He was very honest, and rather brave I think.'

He wasn't kidding! There would be murder when Neil found out.

'I have spoken to Neil and I'm going to see his parents this afternoon. I don't like bullying and I don't like dishonesty.'

He looked at me for a moment or two before continuing. 'I'm also a bit disappointed that you didn't feel able to tell me the truth. Are you afraid of Neil?'

What a daft question – didn't he know we were talking foxes and rabbits?

'I don't know,' I mumbled.

'I hope you'll tell me if anything happens again,' he said. 'Will you?'

'Yes, Mr Doyle,' I answered. I would have said anything to get out of his office.

'OK John, you can go.'

Breathing a sigh of relief. I made for the door, before pausing. A thought had occurred to me. 'Will Gerry be punished?' I asked.

'And miss the match, you mean?' asked Doyley.

I nodded.'

'No, he won't be punished. I think it took a bit of courage to come to me. By the way, what do you think of the idea of a joint North City team?'

I turned to face Doyley. 'Do you really want to know?'

'Yes. Be as honest as you like.'

'I think it'll lose us the match.'

'Wouldn't that be worth it to stop all this gang nonsense?' asked Doyley.

I grimaced. Chance would be a fine thing.

TWELVE

Defeat

'NOT BABYSITTING TODAY?' JEERED A COUPLE OF THE Bride Lane kids.

Gerry glared. 'No,' he muttered. 'The kids are at home.'

'This was one stupid idea,' grumbled Danny Skinner. He was sitting next to Gary Roberts. The other Bride Lane boys sat behind them. The 'team' was divided into two warring tribes.

'Agreed,' said Gerry, 'But we're stuck with it so stop moaning.'

He stared sullenly out of the window of the mini bus at the Lancashire countryside.

'Are you lot quarrelling again?' Goof shouted from the driver's seat.'

'No,' said Danny Skinner.

'Yes,' snapped Mr Crawford, Tony's dad.

'Then stop it,' Goof ordered.

'Keep your hair on,' said Danny.

Goof gave an ill-tempered snort.

For the next five minutes you could have cut the atmosphere with a knife. It was frostier than a penguin's bottom.

'This is it, lads,' Goof announced as we turned into an avenue of poplars.

'So where's the school?' asked Gary Roberts.

'There,' said Gerry. 'The other side of that pond.'

'It looks like something out of the Addams family,' remarked Tony.

'And they really pay to come here?' gasped Gerry, staring at the Victorian building.

'They do that,' said Goof.

'Hello,' Danny interrupted. 'Who's this?'

A tall lad waved us down. 'Are you here for the match?' he asked.

'That's right,' said Goof. 'This is the North City team.'

'You can park over there.'

'Purple blazers!' gasped Richie. 'Fancy wearing them.'

'We'd look like a load of damsons,' Gerry added.

As we stood there looking around the grounds, we were greeted by a tall, mustacheoed man.

'Mr Doyle?' he asked.

'No,' said Goof. 'I'm afraid Mr Doyle had a prior engagement. I'm Mr Scarry. I'm responsible for sport.'

'I'm pleased to meet you. My name is Mr Seymour. I'm the head teacher here at The Norton.'

'Pleased to meet you,' said Goof. 'This is Gerry McEvilly, our team captain.'

Gerry shook Mr Seymour's hand self-consciously.

'You may change here,' said Mr Seymour, pointing to the changing rooms. 'Good luck, everybody.'

'They're like a bunch of stuffed dummies,' said Gerry, as we jogged onto the pitch.

Goof overheard the comment. 'It's called well-behaved,' he sighed. 'I don't suppose that would mean much to you lot.' After sorting out the second scuffle of the day between Tony Crawford and Gerry Roberts he was getting more than a bit short-tempered.

—— 67 ——

I cast a glance at the ranks of plum-coloured blazers. Gerry was right; never had so little noise been made by so many.

The second leg back in Liverpool would be a different story.

As we took our positions ready for the kick off, Gerry had a go at encouraging the team. 'Right lads,' he said, 'this is for the Martyrs. Give it all you've got.'

'For the Martyrs, is it?' sneered Danny. 'Forget it.'

'For North City, then,' I said, wincing at Gerry's lack of thought. Danny strode away shaking his head.

'This doesn't look good,' I said as I joined Gerry in the centre circle.

'Doyley and his stupid ideas,' he snorted.

We won the toss and kicked off. The first few minutes told us that this Norton lot were going to be no pushover. They were fast, competitive and they were on their own turf.

'Watch that big lad,' Gerry told Gary Roberts, pointing out one of Norton's twin strikers.

'Watch him yourself,' snapped Gary, turning his back.

Twenty minutes had gone before we got our first decent chance. Danny beat his marker and took the ball to the byeline.

'Cross it!' cried Gerry, who was unmarked.'Far post.'

Danny looked up, checked, then rolled it inside to one of the other Bride Lane lads. It was a useless ball. He was marked by two defenders and they gratefully hustled it clear.

'Danny!' yelled Gerry. 'Didn't you see me on the far post?'

'I saw you,' Danny answered bluntly, before racing back downfield to intercept a Norton attack.

I looked in Goof's direction. He was talking to Tony Crawford, who was sub. They were shaking their heads.

The same thing happened again five minutes later. This

time Gary had the ball in mid-field. Norton had closed down everybody except me, but did Gary pass it? No way. He tried to find Danny and gave it away. The Norton full back pounced on the ball and laid it off to his right. Their big striker hit it sweetly with his left foot. One – nil.

'If we're going to pull this one out of the fire,' I told Gerry, 'then we're going to have to play as a team.'

'Tell that to Danny,' he replied sadly.

At half-time we did try to tell that to Danny, but he just didn't want to know.

The second half began as the first had ended. Every move broke down in utter confusion. Suddenly, the North City team had their heads down. It was sinking in that we were on a hiding to nothing.

I was trotting back from yet another unsuccessful attack when I heard Tony Crawford's voice from the sideline. 'John, behind you.'

I spun round to see two Norton attackers breaking. Gary was stranded yards behind them. I tried to intercept but I was wrong-footed and crumpled to the ground as the taller boy took the ball on.

I rolled onto my stomach in time to see him round Richie's despairing dive and slot the ball home.

Gerry ran across to Danny. 'Oh, come on, Danny' he pleaded. 'They're two up.'

'Get lost,' said Danny.

He was just walking away from us when one of the Norton kids jogged past.

'Good schools in Liverpool, aren't they?' he chuckled. 'I've heard they're all approved.'

Danny stood rooted to the spot for a second, then set off after his tormentor. I recognized the look on his face. So did Gerry. He dived into Danny's path. 'Don't be stupid,' he begged. 'That's what he wants you to do.'

'That's right,' I agreed. 'That joke's so old it's got whiskers. Can't you just forget it?'

Danny was in no mood to forget it. He shoved Gerry out of his way. 'Don't push it, McEvilly.'

As play resumed I could see Goof standing on the touch-line. He was pointing to his watch.

'Just ten minutes to go,' he shouted. 'Try to keep it down to two.'

Hardly were the words out of his mouth than Norton broke again. It was the boy who'd skitted Danny, and Danny was in hot pursuit.

'Close him down.' Gerry screamed.

I winced. I knew exactly how Danny closed players down, but there was nothing I could do but watch as he powered in.

'Break his leg, Dan!' somebody yelled behind me.

Danny didn't break his leg, but he did just about everything else. Tugging the Norton kid's shirt he pulled him off balance before falling heavily on top of him.

'He kicked me!' shrieked Danny's victim.

'I never,' Danny protested. 'It was an accident.'

'That foul,' said Mr Seymour, bending down to examine his player, 'was no accident. What have you got here Mr Scarry, a school or a crowd of hooligans?'

For once Goof was lost for words.

'Are you all right, lad?' he mumbled finally.

I watched the Norton kid hobbling to his feet. Danny had worked him over good style and he was lucky still to be on the pitch.

'Is that your idea of football?' demanded Gerry.

'So what if it is?' Danny retorted.

'So Norton can have this game,' said Gerry. 'I'd rather lose than win like that.'

'Did you mean that?' I asked as we made a wall for the free kick.

'Too right I did,' said Gerry. 'They'll think we're all animals in Liverpool.'

The shot cannoned off Gary. It was the last real attack

from either side and we trooped off the pitch 2 – 0 losers. It was our first defeat in six games and it left a bitter taste.

'Oh well,' said Goof. 'It isn't the end of the world. There's always the replay.'

'Not with them there isn't,' said Gerry.

'Meaning?' asked Danny.

'Meaning you make me ashamed to come from Liverpool.' Gerry's eyes were flashing and I knew he meant exactly what he said.

Danny glared for a moment then flew at Gerry, grabbing his shirt. Gerry instinctively held onto Danny's arms to defend himself.

'Just look at them,' sneered one of the passing Norton team, as Goof separated Danny and Gerry. 'If they're not fighting us, they're fighting each other. No wonder they're such a bunch of losers.'

We all froze at the remark. There was nothing we could say. He was right.

THIRTEEN

A lost cause

'I JUST HOPE DOYLEY'S HAPPY NOW,' RAGED GERRY. 'That's it, isn't it? Two nil down and half the side playing a different game to the rest of us.'

'It could be worse,' I said reassuringly.

'How?' Gerry cried. 'Just tell me how.'

'Well,' I said. 'It is only two-nil. We could still pull that back.'

Gerry was incredulous. 'The way Bride Lane are playing? Grow up, John.'

'They might still come around,' I told him.

'And you really believe that?'

I thought for a moment. 'No.'

'Neither do I. It's a lost cause.'

Gerry was really fired up. He'd been like this ever since we left the mini bus outside school. I looked up at the tower blocks silhouetted against the watery early evening sunlight.

'I wonder what it's like going to that school,' I said.

'Beats me,' said Gerry, 'but I bet they've all got nice houses. I bet their parents pay the insurance too.'

'That's a bit unfair,' I argued. 'Your dad didn't ask to be put out of work.'

'And I didn't ask to be born in North stinking City!'

'It won't always be like this,' I said.

'Won't it?' Gerry cried. 'And what's going to change?'

'You might play professional,' I said. 'My dad says you're good enough.'

'That was always my dream,' said Gerry. 'Take those kids from The Norton. So what if they lose? It's just a game to them. They've got lots of other things to look forward to. What have I got? Football's not a game to me. It's everything. You know that feeling when you score?'

'Yes,' I said, 'I know what you mean.'

'You know something,' Gerry continued, hardly taking any notice of me. 'My dad used to say football was my ticket out of North City. I believed him too. I thought I'd be like the top players, driving a flash car with my name on the side. Well, he doesn't talk about it any more. He doesn't even come to see me play.

I didn't know what to say.

'I'd do anything to win that game,' Gerry added after a few moments. 'Just imagine it, a bunch of scallies like us beating that lot. It'd really be something. Even my dad would sit up and take notice.'

'Yes,' I said. 'It would really be something.'

Gerry and I looked at each other, then turned the corner into his road.

'I'll drop my kit of,' said Gerry. 'Then we can go off somewhere.'

'Such as?'

'The park? Yours?'

'I'll have to call in at home anyway,' I said. 'I don't want to carry this bag round all night.'

Gerry had his key and let us in. His dad was in his usual place, stuck in front of the telly.

'How did you do?' he asked casually, without taking his eyes off the screen.

'It was like a red rag to a bull.

—— 73 ——

'What do you care?' snapped Gerry.

'You what?'

'What's up?' Gerry answered. 'Deaf as well as useless?'

His dad leapt to his feet.

'Leave it, Ger,' I hissed.

'Why should I?' Gerry replied. 'He wanted to know, so I'm telling him. We lost Dad, but what do you care?'

'Don't speak to me like that!' his dad barked.

Gerry gave a bitter, mocking laugh. 'We lost Dad. Two nil. It was embarrassing. We spent more time arguing among ourselves than playing the opposition.'

Mr McEvilly was furious, his eyes flashing and his body coiled as if ready to lash out at any moment. 'Don't come in here shouting the odds at me.'

'Why not?'

'Because I just said so, that's why.'

Father and son faced each other, their faces tense and bitter. I watched anxiously, wondering whether Mr McEvilly was going to hit Gerry.

'All I want,' said Gerry, 'is to have somebody on my side, that's right, somebody completely on my side. I used to think it was the Delaneys, but I was wrong about that. There was a time I even thought it was you, but John here's the only one who's ever stuck by me. The only one.'

With that, Gerry threw his bag across the room and made for the front door. As he did his mum walked in from the shops with Kieran and Susie.

'What's all the shouting in aid of?' she asked. 'I could hear you half-way up the street.'

Gerry stared at her for a moment then pushed past.

'Gerry,' she said. 'I asked you a question.'

'Did you Mum?' he retorted as he walked down the front path. 'I wasn't listening.'

Those were his last words.

'What on earth was that all about?' demanded Gerry's

dad as his son stamped away down the front path. 'Is something wrong?'

I stood there for a moment or two. 'Why not ask Gerry?' I said as I walked away. Even before I reached the pavement I could hear a furious argument erupting between Mr and Mrs McEvilly and Kieran and Susie crying. Gerry broke into a run and I followed him out along the main road towards my house.

'They'll kill you when you go home,' I said.

'Maybe,' said Gerry. 'Who cares?'

'Me for a start.'

'Who else?'

I tried to make a joke out of it. 'Goof would be short of a captain.'

Gerry gave me a smile but he wasn't fooling me. His eyes were brimming with tears and his voice was thick with hurt and frustration.

'Do you want to play Space Raiders?' I asked.

'Yes,' said Gerry, rubbing his eyes with his sleeve. 'Why not?'

As we pushed our way through the back gate we could see Dad examining the pile of bricks which was supposed to be a barbecue.

'Still not done it, Dad?' I asked.

'No,' he answered. 'I'm doing something wrong.'

'You're right there,' I observed.

'Do you think your dad would do it for me?' Dad asked Gerry.

Gerry looked at the bricks. 'He might,' he said, 'but don't expect me to ask him.'

Dad stared after Gerry.

'What's up with him?' he asked.

'Well,' I began, 'for a start we lost two – nil. Then there's the Delaneys. They're after his blood. Oh, and he's fallen out with his parents.'

'I see,' said Dad. 'Is that all?'

FOURTEEN

All together now?

GERRY PUSHED THE PIECE OF PAPER ACROSS THE DESK. I gave him a puzzled look. 'Read it,' he whispered, as Mrs King handed out the history topic folders. Unfolding the single sheet I saw a clumsily-drawn gravestone bearing the legend: *Gerry McEvilly RIP. So end all traitors.*

'You're not taking it seriously, are you?' I asked, stealing a glance three rows back at a smirking Neil Delaney.

'It's my neck,' whispered Gerry. 'Of course I'm taking it seriously. You know what they're like.'

'Then why don't you take this to Doyley?'

'Did you say something, John?' asked Mrs King.

'No Miss,' said John Turner.

'I meant you, John Ryan,' said Mrs King.

'Me Miss?' I answered. 'No Miss.'

Running her fingers over a page of notes, Mrs King began to write on the board. Something about Helots and Hoplites. I hadn't got the hang of the Ancient Greeks at all. We were saved from the Spartans by a knock at the door. It was Doyley.

'Good morning Year Six,' he said.

'Good morning Mr Doyle,' we chorused.

'Would you mind if I had a short talk to the class, Mrs King?' he asked.

'They're all yours,' she replied.

'Now,' said Mr Doyle, perching on the desk. 'You all know that we are playing host this afternoon to The Norton School in the second leg of a friendly.'

There was a loud snort of laughter behind me. It was bound to be Neil.

'It's attitudes like that, Neil Delaney,' snapped Mr Doyle, 'that I have come to talk about. The last two matches our team has been involved in have been bad-tempered affairs. I am particularly concerned at the conduct of one boy over at The Norton.'

'But he was from Bride Lane,' interrupted Tony Crawford.

'That's right,' said Richie Harris. 'It wasn't our fault.'

'I'm quite aware which boy is to blame for a particularly nasty foul,' said Doyley, 'and he's been made sub because of the incident.' He took a deep breath. 'I think I'm right, however, in saying that all was not well between our boys and their Bride Lane team mates.'

I glanced across at Gerry.

'Well?' demanded Doyley. 'Am I right?'

A few of us nodded.

'Then what I am looking for is team spirit and sportsmanship,' said Doyley. 'For a start you can clap their team onto the pitch.'

'You're kidding!' said Neil.

'No Neil, I am not kidding,' said Doyley. 'I think it's the least we can do. What's more, once the match is underway I don't want to see any dirty play or hear any bad language from the spectators. The whole Junior Department from our school and Bride Lane are watching the game and I expect to see you all on your best behaviour.'

He gave Mrs King a thin smile and left the room.

'That,' Gerry murmured, 'is a man living in a dream world.'

'This is embarrassing,' I whispered to Gerry.

'I know,' he answered, 'but Doyley's watching us like a hawk. Just keep clapping.'

Goof was refereeing the match and called Gerry and The Norton skipper into the centre circle.

'Call,' said Goof.

'Heads,' said The Norton captain.

'Heads it is,' Goof told him.

'We'll kick off,' said The Norton captain.

I scanned the touch line to find Dad. He waved and I waved back. Just past him I spotted Danny Skinner sitting on the substitutes' bench. He didn't look happy.

From the whistle The Norton went onto the attack, winning two corners in quick succession. Gary Roberts finally intercepted, but refused the obvious pass to Tony Crawford and gave it away on the edge of the box. The Norton attacker's shot was wild and we were lucky not to be punished for the mistake.

'Oh, not again,' Gerry complained.

'Just play, McEvilly,' said Gary.

'Please,' said Gerry. 'I mean, who wins if we fight each other?'

Gary just brushed Gerry aside. Gerry looked across at me. I held out my arms in a gesture of despair.

It was a scrappy match for most of the first half. Thanks to the grudge between Bride Lane and the Martyrs we could hardly string two passes together. As for The Norton, they seemed to think they'd got it sewn up and they weren't stretching themselves.

'Well,' said Gerry as half-time approached. 'If we've got to do it on our own, then that's exactly what we'll do.'

He picked up the ball just inside The Norton half and

powered down the left flank, taking two defenders with him. All of a sudden there was a rage in him. Nothing and nobody was going to make a loser out of him. I made ground to give him a target. Sure enough he found me and I side-stepped a hasty tackle to find myself on the edge of the box with one man to beat. As the goalkeeper moved to block a possible shot I glimpsed Tony Crawford bursting into the area. Checking to the right I crossed the ball and watched with glee as Tony dived forward to head it in.

'Goal!'

The celebration was short-lived, however. Tony had collided with the post and hadn't got up.

'Tony,' I asked, 'Are you all right?'

He didn't answer. His face was very pale.

'Mr Scarry,' I shouted. 'Tony's hurt.'

Soon everybody was crowding round. 'It's not his head, thank goodness,' said Goof. 'It's his shoulder. Come on son, on your feet.'

As Tony was helped over to the touch line, I saw Danny getting ready to come on in his place.

'Wonderful,' said Gerry. 'Another wrecker on the field and just when things were looking up.'

Stung by the goal The Norton piled on the pressure. They were determined to get the equaliser before half-time. With a couple of minutes to go the pressure paid off. Gary had the ball on the half-way line and was looking for someone to pass it to.

As usual he turned down the chance to set up Gerry and tried an ambitious pass across the field. A Norton player easily intercepted it and presented their tall striker with a perfectly flighted ball. He hit it on the volley. 1 – 1.

'Well, thanks a bunch!' I cried angrily at Gary.

'Leave him alone,' said Danny intervening.

'What's this?' asked one of the Norton players. 'Fighting among yourselves again. That should make it easy.'

'You know what?' Gerry said. 'He's right. I don't know why I bothered even trying. It's hopeless.'

With that he walked away looking utterly defeated.

We'd only just re-started when Goof blew for half-time. With Goof acting as ref, it was Doyley who gave us the half-time pep talk. He went on a bit about playing for one another and forgetting old differences, then raised his voice angrily. 'Am I boring you Gerry?' he asked.

Gerry was staring down the touch line.

'I said,' Doyley repeated. 'Am I boring you?'

'What's that?' asked Gerry. 'Yes, I suppose so, Mr Doyle.'

'I give up,' said Doyley. 'Just try to play together as a team, lads.'

I tried to discover what Gerry had been staring at. It didn't take long. There, just by the half way line stood Mr and Mrs McEvilly with Kieran and Susie.

'Well, there you go Ger,' I said. 'Maybe you ought to tell them how you feel a bit more often.'

Gerry walked over to his parents.

'Sorry I've let you down,' said his dad. 'I just . . .'

'Forget it, Dad,' said Gerry. 'So long as you're here now.'

'Right then,' said Mr McEvilly. 'Go out there and win.'

It was as if Gerry had grown a whole foot taller.

'You know what?' he said. 'That's just what we're going to do.' Then, as an afterthought he added: 'If Bride Lane let us.'

As he jogged to the centre circle he passed Danny.

'Is that your dad?' asked Danny, staring at Mr McEvilly.

'Yes, why?'

I knew exactly why. Danny remembered how Gerry's dad had saved his bacon the time he broke into the garden shed.

'Oh nothing.'

We'd been playing for about five minutes when something very odd happened. Danny had the ball on the centre circle and was looking for supprt. Gerry was free but hadn't even raised his arm to ask for the pass.

'Gerry!' shouted Danny. 'Your ball.'

With that he drifted a cross to Gerry's feet. Gerry was so surprised it took him two tries to bring it under control. Looking up, he saw me in space and chipped it forward. It was only the tall Norton striker coming back to help his defence who cut it out.

'Are you feeling quite all right, Danny?' asked Gerry as he trotted over to take the corner.

'Never better,' said Danny. He turned towards Gerry's dad. 'Maybe it's time we stuck up for our own. I'm not having a bunch of stuck-up face-aches putting us down.'

'So we're going for it?' asked Gerry excitedly.

'What do you think?'

Gerry played the corner short to Danny. Danny held it up for a second to draw the Norton defence then played the one-two. On receiving the return ball he hit it low. I stuck out a foot. 2 – 1.

'You know something,' said Gary. 'We could win this.'

'Correction,' said Gerry. 'We *are* going to win this.'

The Nortons weren't ready to just roll over and die and it was twenty minutes before we got another really clear-cut chance. Richie hoofed the ball the full length of the field and it fell to the lad who'd been taunting us. He fluffed the backpass and punted it right into Gerry's path. Gerry never was one to look a gift horse in the mouth and he lofted the ball over the Norton keeper and into the net. The Norton keeper was livid and let his defender know it.

'Look at them,' Danny said loudly. 'Too busy arguing among themselves to beat us.'

The Norton defender glared at Danny. If looks could kill!

The last quarter of the match was all North City as The Norton tried to keep it at 3 – 3 on aggregate.

'Come on,' Gerry panted as we got a free kick. 'Scallies United.'

Danny was being marked by his arch enemy and they were jostling for position. Gerry knocked it to me and I returned it as he made ground. Danny had just succeeded in giving his man the slip.

'All yours,' shouted Gerry, seeing him a couple of strides clear.

As Danny pushed the ball into the area, the Norton player stretched out a leg and brought Danny down from behind.

'Penalty!' shouted Gerry.

Goof raced in pointing to the spot.

I watched Danny rising to his feet. 'Don't do it, Dan,' I whispered.

'Do what?' asked Danny, as the Norton player retreated to avoid his anger.

'I'm a gentleman.'

'Since when?'

'Since dog food breath over there called me approved.'

'Do you want to take it?' asked Gerry.

'Is coal black?' chuckled Danny.

With a short run-up he confidently slotted the ball home. 4 – 1.

The Norton tried to come at us, but their hearts were no longer in it. Five minuts later Goof blew for full time. That was it; a 4 – 3 victory on aggregate. The roar was loud enough to crack every window in the city.

'We did it,' I yelled, patting Danny on the back.

'Yes,' said Danny, winking at Gerry. 'We did, didn't we?'

'We'll have to do it again some time,' said Gerry. 'Just not too often eh?'

'No,' said Danny. 'I think once is enough.'

Now we just had to wait for the presentation of the shield to the winning team. While Doyley and Mr Seymour droned on about fair play and sportsmanship, I watched Gerry talking excitedly to his mum and dad.

'That's good to see, isn't it?' said my dad.

'Yes,' I said. 'Brilliant.'

We went over to join them.

'They did well, didn't they Barry?' said Dad.

Gerry's dad nodded. 'Yes,' he said. 'Our Gerry could give me a few lessons in life, couldn't you son?'

Gerry just smiled.

'By the way,' said Dad to Mr McEvilly. 'I've got a favour to ask.'

'What's that?'

'You couldn't build me a barbecue, could you?'

Just then Doyley called out Gerry's name.

'Here's the trophy,' he said, handing it over. 'Six months at Bride Lane and six months at English Martyrs. Who's having it first?'

Gerry kissed the shield. 'There you go Dan,' he said.

Danny took the shield with a wry grin.

'Well well,' said Goof loudly, his bald patch gleaming in the sun. 'Now I've seen everything.'

FIFTEEN

Set up

'JUST A MINUTE,' SAID MRS MCEVILLY AS WE REACHED the school gates. 'Where's Gerry?'

I'd been so busy re-living the match to my dad that I didn't even know he'd gone.

'He was here a minute ago,' said Mr McEvilly.

Susie took her thumb out of her mouth with a loud pop. 'He went with a big boy,' she said.

'Big boy,' I repeated. 'What big boy?'

Susie looked around. 'That one,' she said. 'There.' She was pointing at Tony Crawford.

'Tony,' I shouted. 'Did you come for Gerry?'

'That's right,' said Tony. 'Mr Scarry wanted him.'

'There's Mr Scarry talking to Doyley and Mr Seymour. It hardly seemed likely that they'd want any of us hanging round.

'Who gave you the message?' I asked Tony.

'What? Oh, it was Neil.'

'Neil!' the answer hit me like a low-flying hippo. 'I think that goalpost must have scrambled your brains, Tony. Didn't you think it was a bit odd?'

Tony stared at me, his mouth opening and closing like a cod fish.

'Do I have to spell it out?' I yelled. 'Since when did any of the teachers trust Neil with a message? It'd be like asking Dracula to run a blood bank.'

The cod fish was still short of answers.

'Where was Mr Scarry supposed to be, anyway?' I demanded.

'The changing rooms,' mumbled Tony. 'Neil said he was in the changing rooms. Sorry John.'

My heart was thudding. I could hardly think straight. 'If anything happens to Gerry, you will be.'

Without a word to anybody I was on my toes and heading for the changing rooms. I could hear Dad and the McEvillys calling my name but I wasn't going to stop for anybody. The Delaneys would have already got Gerry. I reached the side entrance to school and tugged the door handle. It was no use – it had been locked.

'What's up, John?' came a voice. 'Have you forgotten something?'

I spun round. It was Danny. Gary was with him.

'It's Gerry,' I panted. 'The Delaneys have got him.'

I didn't stop to explain further. There was only one idea in my head. Find Gerry.

I ran round the outside of the school to the front entrance.

'Gerry!' I shouted as I burst through the doors.

There was no answer. I ran down the corridor and through the hall. Taking a deep breath I opened the door and stepped into Year Six's cloakroom. Nothing. My mind was racing. That's when I heard voices from the Year Five cloakroom. Of course, that's where The Norton had got changed.

'Gerry!' I called as I ran through the hall.

As I flung open the door I was met by Dean Brewer, Steve and Neil had Gerry pinned against the wall.

'What's this?' asked Steve. 'Two for the price of one.'

'Come on then,' said Dean. 'Now you're here what are you going to do?'

Suddenly my neck was burning. What could I do?

'Run!' cried Gerry. 'There's no use both of us getting a kicking.'

'Oh no,' said Dean, blocking my way. 'You're not going anywhere.'

'Leave him alone,' said Gerry. 'It's me you want.'

'Shut it, McEvilly,' said Steve, twisting Gerry's arm.

Gerry winced with pain, but he wasn't about to keep quiet. 'I'm not scared of you,' he told them. 'Look at your gang now. What happened to the others then? They weren't impressed when they saw you begging Graham Skinner to leave you alone, were they?'

Steve was incensed. Shoving Gerry to the ground he stood astride him. 'You know something,' he said. 'You've got too much mouth.'

Even though he was on the floor, Gerry still wasn't done. Pushing himself free of Steve, he started kicking at his tormentors. 'Do what you like,' he yelled. 'You're finished. Nobody cares what you do any more. You're finished.'

'Finished, are we?' said Steve. 'Come on Neil, let's show him who's finished.'

That's when I heard the door creak.

'I wouldn't do that, Delaney,' declared Danny as he stepped into the changing rooms, followed by Gary.

'What's this?' jeered Dean. 'Kiddies' outing. What do you think you runts can do?'

I weighed the balance of forces. It was four onto three. But Steve and Dean were four years older than us. They were taller and stronger. I didn't have any doubts who would win if it came to the crunch.

'Come on then,' said Dean. 'Come and have a go. You don't bother us.'

Danny didn't bother trading insults. Instead he turned a bench over in the path of our opponents. Taking advantage of the diversion Gerry was up like a shot and first out of the door. Suddenly the rest of us were following suit.

'I'll have you for this,' yelled Steve, stumbling over the upturned furniture.

'Leg it!' cried Danny as Dean made a grab for us.

We didn't need telling twice. A split-second later we were tearing across the hall.

'Out of the way!' cried Gerry as Mr McGurk the caretaker arrived to find out what all the noise was about.

With the Delaneys gaining we wrenched open the front door and raced onto the playing field.

'Stop!' cried Gerry suddenly.

'What's up?' asked Danny.

'Look,' said Gerry. 'They've got Gary.'

It was true. They must have caught him as he tried to get out of the door.

'Right,' said Steve, shoving Gary against the wall. 'Give me McEvilly and the rest of you can go.'

'Tell him to get lost,' croaked Gary, struggling against Steve's arm lock. We stood facing the Delaneys, uncertain what to do next.

'Give yourself up, McEvilly,' said Dean.

'OK,' came a voice behind us,' I will.'

Gerry spun round. 'Dad!'

'Now lads,' said Gerry's dad. 'You've had your fun. Let him go and clear off.'

Behind Mr McEvilly I could see Gerry's mum and my dad.

'I'm waiting,' said Mr McEvilly.

Steve looked Gerry's dad up and down.

'It's not over,' he snarled, grudgingly releasing Gary.

'What was that, Delaney?' snapped Mr McEvilly taking a couple of steps forward.

'You heard,' said Steve, sounding braver than he looked.

'Oh, it's over all right' said Gerry. 'It ended on that field. Didn't you notice? For once we were all together.'

'That's right,' said Danny. 'It's over Steve.'

'Does your Graham know that?' snapped Dean.

'No,' Danny answered. 'But he soon will.'

Dean and the Delaney brothers turned their backs and walked away.

In the silence that followed I sidled up to Gerry. 'Got enough people on your side now?' I asked.

'Not yet,' said Gerry with a smile, 'but it'll do for a start.'